The Artist

By

Angelo Marcos

ISBN-13: 978-1479319275
ISBN-10: 1479319279

About the Author

Angelo Marcos is a writer, comedian and actor, and a graduate of both law and psychology.

He has performed stand up comedy all over the UK, and has acted in numerous short films and theatrical productions.

He co-wrote the musical 'Love and Marriage' which was performed at the Edinburgh Festival, and also contributed to the Royal British Legion book 'In the Footsteps of War'.

His articles and short stories have been published both online and in print, and his novels and short story collections are available in both ebook and paperback formats.

You can find his website at **www.angelomarcos.com**

What others are saying about 'The Artist':

"a well paced, well-written and exciting novel, with an incredible twist at the end that few could possibly anticipate"

- *DustJacketGang.com*

"a real page turner, with twists that will stun you. Thoroughly enjoyed this one!"

- *Iconicgifts.com*

"...similar to Shutter Island in that it causes the reader to reconsider a number of events in the book...a tense psychological thriller"

- *Parikiaki.com*

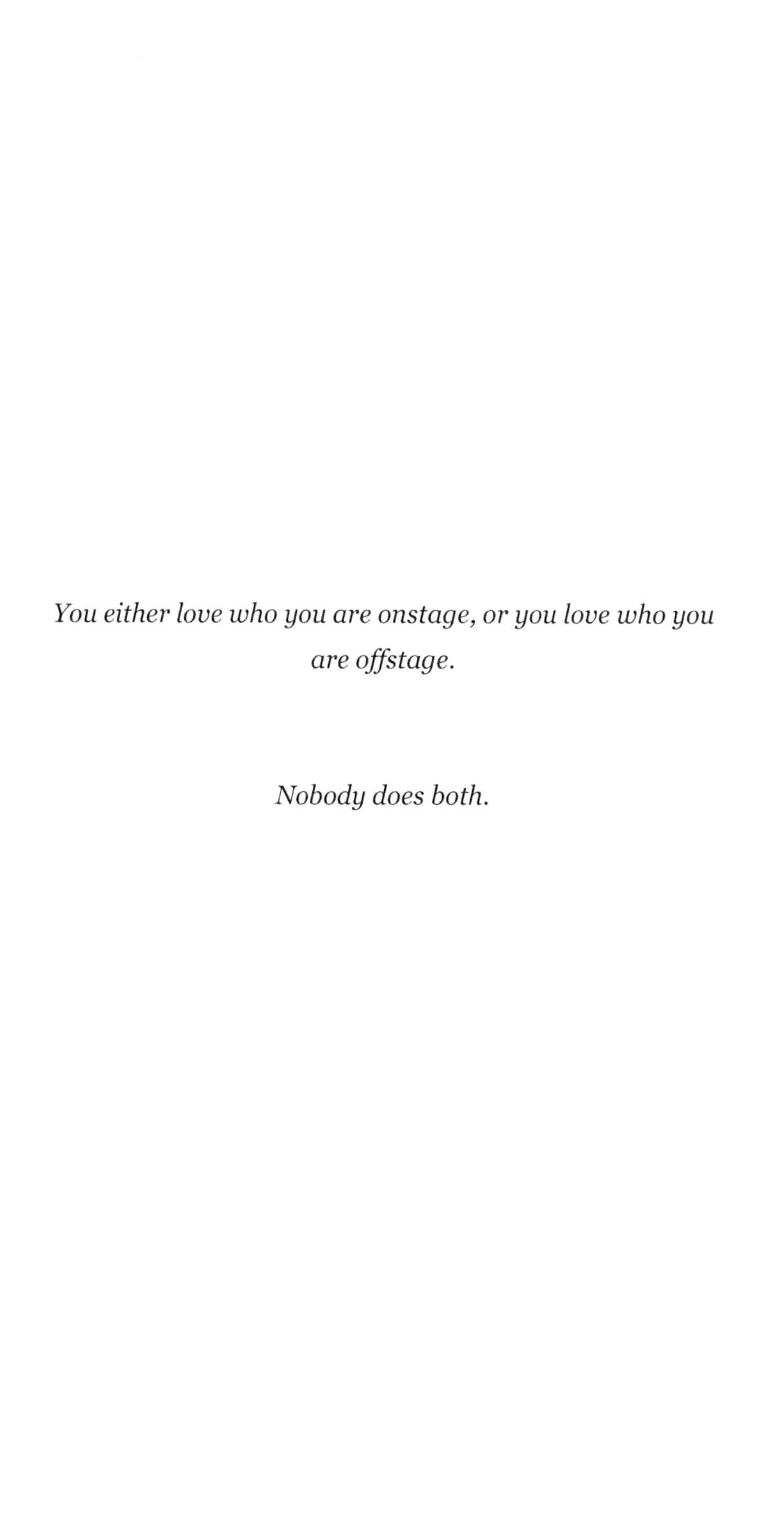

You either love who you are onstage, or you love who you are offstage.

Nobody does both.

One

The shrill tone of the alarm pierces the air like a needle into skin.

The girl stirs, her barely conscious brain slowly booting up like a well-worn computer. She blinks, her senses blurred by those first few moments after sleep. Those seconds where the day, date – sometimes even the location – are elusive. Unreachable.

But this time is different.

This time everything is unreachable for longer than a few seconds and the blurriness becomes confusion becomes fear. This time she's strapped to a rickety wooden chair and can feel thick, hard tape pushing against her mouth. This time panic has her in its grip, the merciless claws cutting through the meat and lodging solidly into bone.

The alarm stops.

She keeps her head down and tries to formulate her thoughts, terrified of what she might see if she lifts her gaze.

With every passing second the silence grows more deafening than the alarm that preceded it.

Her eyes focus on her shins and she sees the thick, dirty cords binding her to the legs of the creaky wooden chair.

Without the constant tone of the alarm ricocheting around her head she realises the only thing she can hear is her blood – surely more adrenalin than haemoglobin now -

rushing in her ears. Coupled with that is the horrific rhythm of her breath violently being sucked into and blown out of her nose. A tornado whooshing back and forth through a maze, frantically searching for a way out.

She wonders where she could be. And *when* she could be – she didn't even know how long she'd been asleep.

Waves of fear seep out of every pore of her body.

A stray thought enters her mind. *Is it seeping out, or is it seeping in?*

Her heartrate ratchets up, amplifying the sound of the blood-ocean in her ears. She wonders just how fast the human heart can beat, feeling as though if it got any faster the friction would start a fire in her chest. An inferno racing through her body with the same relentless ferocity of the adrenalin careering through her veins.

Her father's voice suddenly explodes from somewhere inside her head. His deep smokers' drawl from fourteen years ago, that summer when she was a little girl and too scared to dive into the hotel pool. The first holiday together since the divorce, the one he'd promised to take her on for being such a brave girl. The one where he'd said he'd teach her to swim.

"Just relax baby," he'd said in that specific tone that fathers reserve for their little girls. "The worst thing to do as a swimmer is to panic. It's true. Nine times out of ten, if a person finds themselves in the middle of the ocean and in trouble, it's not the water that gets them, it's their own minds. They start to panic, then they stop thinking properly and breathing properly and end up going under. Don't worry baby, just keep your focus and it won't happen, I promise. Just relax, Susie. Keep your head and you'll be just fine. I'm right here baby."

But you're not right here, Daddy. I'm on my own now.

Feeling the panic rising somehow concentrates her thoughts. Her father was right, she needs to keep her focus.

I can keep it, Daddy. I will.

She takes a deep breath and slowly lifts her head. As she does so, a stranger in front of her does the same and she realises that the entire top half of the wall in front of her is a mirror. She sees now the tight black tape forced around her mouth, and the restraints binding her upper body to the chair. She takes another breath, and swallows down the fear before it engulfs her.

By turning her head and looking at the reflection in the mirror, she studies the room. A sparse white cell with painted brick walls and a stained cement floor. For the first time she notices an imposing iron door to her right, and somewhere in her brain a connection is made as the synapses fire.

I'm in a police cell.

Not that she has ever been in one, but this is how she remembers them from television and films. And she'd watched a lot of those.

It was a textbook interrogation room. An empty room with a one-way mirror, a bare light-bulb and a rickety chair. Her attention drawn to the chair, she realises how unstable it is. As though at any given time it might break under her weight, slamming her into the floor.

The thought that she is in a police cell allows her to relax slightly. Not completely, but enough to keep the rising nausea at bay. Whatever else may happen here, at least she wouldn't be drowning in her own vomit.

Police have rules, they don't hurt innocent people. I'll tell them what they want to know and then I can leave.

The words sound hollow as her subconscious minds picks up on what her conscious mind doesn't. Police don't tie a suspect's arms and legs to a chair, or gag their mouth, or wake them with an alarm. And why had she been asleep?

She feels the negative emotion accompanying negative subconscious thought. Those times where, in the deepest recesses of a person's mind, they realise something terrible but don't yet allow themselves to formulate what it is.

She looks again at the mirror.

An interrogation room. What could I possibly know that the police would want?

For the past three months she'd been working for a marketing company, making calls to businesses and annoying them with surveys. Before that she'd been a waitress, and before that she'd worked in a bar. In between all this there'd been acting jobs – if that wasn't too grandiose a term - with the occasional modelling job thrown in too. She lived alone, hadn't had a boyfriend or been associated with anyone who could possibly have been a criminal.

At least, I don't think I have.

She even made sure her phone bill was always paid on time, or did when she could actually afford to pay it. Hardly a prime suspect for a case that warranted an interrogation. Especially one like this.

What would I know that they would want?

Think! Focus!

This is too important to start ge –

Her thoughts are interrupted by a voice. A distorted, disembodied growl booming from some unseen speaker, the vibrations ricocheting off the walls of the cell.

"The timer starts now. You have fifteen minutes. Make it count."

In her mind a swarm of questions attack like hornets.

Who was that?

Why is there a timer?

Fifteen minutes?

What the fuck is going to happen after fifteen minutes?!

The panic rises and her eyes lose focus as her heartbeat gets faster and harder and louder and the sweat from her forehead runs into her eyes and drips onto the floor. The restraints feel tighter and her wrists bleed as she struggles to break free and the back of her neck burns and her head swims and she can't breathe anymore and –

NO! Focus!

What is this? What could be happening here?!

She uses all the reserves she has left to focus her mind. A laser cutting through thick fog.

Controlling what she can, she takes slow, deliberate breaths.

Start with the voice. Who did it sound like? An ex-boyfriend? Doubtful.

The voice was distorted so it could've been a woman and not a man anyway. Could it really have been a woman? Why would a woman do this to me?

Why would anybody do this to anyone?

Who then? A kidnapper? Why would a kidnapper go to all this trouble just to kill me after fifteen minutes?

Kill me...

Oh, please, no...

She suddenly becomes acutely aware of the tape on her mouth, and the fact that if these are the last moments of her life then she is unable to even utter a last word – surely the right of any person. The right to sum up the life lived, the lessons learned. The right to impart some kind of wisdom, or at the very least tie up the experiences of the preceding years. The farewell to this world before leaving for the next -

STOP!

I am not going to die!

Keep it together. Breathe.

Panic rising, heartbeat racing, tears falling –

Her father's voice bursts into her head.

Relax, baby. Think straight, baby. Breathe straight, baby. I'm right here. I'm right here...

Anger suddenly explodes within her. Rage in its purest, basest form. A mother confronting the man who murdered her child. A husband protecting his wife.

No! I am not going to die here in this fucking place! Fuck you!

She kicks her legs and tenses her arms, trying desperately to loosen the restraints. Her once-beautiful face becomes an ugly rictus of panic and desperation, as she as she grimaces and contorts in an attempt to break the tape covering her mouth. She strains and jolts her head, swishing left and right until her neck burns, as if the sweat pouring from her hair and head isn't sweat at all but acid, eroding her skin all the way down.

Images of her life flash through her mind. Not chronologically like she'd seen in a million movie death scenes, but randomly. The powdered chicken and vegetable soup she's left in her locker at work. Ready for lunch tomorrow. Low-fat, high-protein, part of her new diet. Her mum keeps telling her she's beautiful as she is, she doesn't need to diet. But she does, actresses *always* need to diet. A few weeks from now she has an audition for a part she is pretty much ready to kill for – *don't say kill, no I can say it if I want it doesn't matter because I AM NOT GOING TO DIE HERE* - and she most definitely is not going to run the risk of being told she needs to lose weight. Not after all the work she's put in. Acting classes, kissing arses of everyone remotely important she's ever met. "I'm not missing this opportunity for anything, mum, I'll live on nothing but water and ambition for the next month if I have to."

More images. The birthday party where she got ill. The driving lesson where she finally got the hang of driving a manual, after two months of driving her best friend's automatic. The time she helped her neighbour with her garden and got extra pocket money and praise for her efforts – "Hilary, Anthony, that's an amazing little girl you've got there." Last Christmas when her sister couldn't make it because she was dancing in a show in Switzerland.

Struggling with the restraints. Getting nowhere. A slight trickle of blood from her left wrist where the restraints are slicing into her flesh.

Don't panic, baby. We can do this, baby. I'm right here, baby.

More images and more images. The soup again.

I need to get the soup, I have to keep my diet to get the part. Please, just loosen a little bit. Let me get through this, let me get out of this place.

Tears again. Streaming down her cheeks. Crazy thoughts.

Maybe the tears can loosen the tape, maybe I'll be able to scream. Please Daddy, Mummy, I'm sorry for everything. I know I haven't been the perfect daughter and I could've worked harder at school and I should've got a better job, I should've helped all the times you asked, I should've come with you to see Steven that day. I never meant to hurt any of you. I love you. I love you. I'm sorry. I'm so sorry. Please...

A noise from the door, metal sliding on metal, the sound ricocheting around the cell. A small shaft of light falls harshly on the side of Susie's face. She turns as far as she can and sees a gun barrel being pushed through the newly lit gap, scraping metal on metal again. A gunshot rings through the cell as the sound of a bullet ripping through bone and skin and brain and hair joins the cacophony.

Then, silence.

Susie - Hilary and Anthony's amazing little girl - was dead.

The production has begun.

Two

The shrill tone of the alarm pierces the air like a needle into skin.

The girl stirs, her barely conscious brain slowly booting up like a well-worn computer. She blinks, her senses blurred by those first few moments after sleep. Those seconds where the day, date – sometimes even the location – are elusive. Unreachable.

Then she remembered - it was Monday. And as she drifted further from sleep and closer to reality, she realised that she couldn't hear an alarm at all, merely the phone ringing.

Kaylin Bellos smiled to herself as she relaxed back into the mattress, stretching like a cat in the hot summer sunshine, and lamenting that if she did own an alarm maybe she wouldn't be late for everything. Not that it mattered very much, unless turning up to school on time was important, and it wasn't. There were more things in life to worry about than getting to registration on time. A lot more things.

Her smile faded.

She took a breath then exhaled deeply, as if trying to remove every trace of air from her lungs. If anyone else was around to hear it they would have remarked that it was a very big sigh for a very small girl. But then, what did they know?

And she wasn't that small, not mentally anyway; people were always telling her she was 'wiser than her years' – for whatever that was worth.

She lay in bed for a while, turning thoughts over in her mind as she analysed - and overanalysed - everything. She considered her life, her future, and all the other things that normally don't concern fourteen-year-old girls, only the *parents* of fourteen-year-old girls.

How are we going to pay the rent? Are they going to cut off the phone again? Have we paid the gas bill or are they going to cut that off again too?

It would be Christmas soon, and while all her school friends excitedly chattered and made lists of all the gifts they wanted, Kaylin would sit silently. There was only one thing she wanted, and that was for her mum to be happy.

Just for a while. It doesn't even have to be for a long time. A week. No, not even a week. A day. A whole day of happiness.

A bittersweet smile passed her lips; the sweet was the fantasy of her mum happy again, the bitter was the knowledge that it was just that – fantasy.

For the millionth time in her life, Kaylin found her emotions weighing her down and then keeping her there, in the same way the lethargy was right now keeping her fixed to her mattress. She felt vaguely tired all the time, affected by emotions that she didn't yet understand. She was too young to understand the psychosomatic effect of stress on the body. Too young to understand that watching the suffering of someone you love is like watching somebody drown from a distance, knowing by the time you get there it'll be too late. You can do nothing but watch, powerless, shouting in vain.

She heard a voice, bursting into life and with a glee that could only mean one thing.

"-audition for that part I wanted. I can't believe it!"

Kaylin looked up at her mum, who had burst into her room brandishing the cordless telephone. The outsider who would remark that Kaylin's sigh was very big for such a small girl would probably also think that was a smile on Kimberley's face, but Kaylin knew different. If you looked carefully it wasn't a smile, but a grimace. A hoping-against-hope mask. The face of a person who has suffered a thousand knocks and bumps, someone who has been disappointed and rejected and let down time and again. A facial expression which was the inevitable result of the stress of having to restrain the destructive beast that was raging within – hope.

It was this beast that did all the damage.

It was this beast that would wreak havoc and stir up emotion, convincing people that they couldn't lose. The voice at the roulette table telling them to keep betting, keep betting, and maybe we'll win it all back and more.

It had to be mercilessly restrained and controlled because if it got loose it would cause *excitement.* And when the ensuing excitement was proved wrong - as it always was - then it would evolve into the largest and most destructive animal of all.

Despair.

And Kaylin knew her mum had felt enough of that for four lifetimes. Oh, she recognised the mask alright. The face of a starving person, trying not to feel happiness at the food being offered because they've learned that it could - and would - be snatched away at any second.

Kaylin, hostage to emotion just like the rest of the human race, couldn't help but allow some of the hope to trickle into her own veins.

"What's the part, mum?" she asked excitedly, not allowing any of the unease she was feeling alongside the excitement to seep into her voice.

I'm quite an actress myself, she thought, as her mum began to tell her about the role with a combination of wild gestures and unrestrained enthusiasm.

Kaylin wasn't fully listening, her focus was on restraining all the little 'buts' and 'are you sures?' that were wont to come out of her mouth at times like this.

"I'll be playing a character called Jemima!"

You might be playing a character called Jemima.

"My agent thinks I'll be perfect for it!"

He always does, mum, then you don't get it and feel horrible about yourself.

"We'll be filming in France!"

Kaylin inhaled sharply, ready to respond aloud this time, with "France? What am I going to do if you're in France? I'm only fourteen, mum!"

She almost had to put her hand over her mouth to stop the words tumbling out by themselves.

"What?" her mum asked, noticing her daughter's sharp intake of breath but blissfully ignorant of her distressed body language. Kaylin may have been mature, but she certainly wasn't sophisticated enough to hide her emotions very well. It was simply fortunate that the times which demanded disguised emotions were also the times when her mum was too excited to notice.

"Nothing," she answered sheepishly, "it's just... I think its good mum. That's all."

Her mum continued talking, still unaware of the conflict raging inside her daughter.

Kaylin watched her mum and suddenly felt like a horrible daughter. Here was her mum, happy, and she was dismissing everything she was saying. Dismissing the very reasons for her happiness. Didn't she wish for her mum's happiness more than anything else? And now here she was denigrating it.

She felt as though she was putting up obstacles at every turn, like a scientist blocking a rat in a maze.

She wasn't doing this aloud,. of course, she had learned a long time ago that voicing her objections got her nowhere when her mum was like this. The retorts were still there, they were just unspoken.

But does that make me a horrible daughter? Or a kind one?

A few minutes later, after she'd gone through the motions of looking pleased for her mum and pretending to believe that *this is it Kaylin, I can feel it this time*, her mum left the room.

Kaylin was alone with the thoughts that had haunted her for years.

What's it like to be normal? With a dad and a secure life and friends and no worries...? That must be something.

She sighed, wondering about the life she didn't have. Then wondering about the one she did have.

She wanted to stay in bed forever, to hide from the world and not have to endure another day. She knew she'd come home to see her mother crying, or drunk, or worse. She wanted to cry as well sometimes, to scream at the world and ask why this had to be her life. As always the sadness, anger and fear all rushed into her at the same time, flooding her with negative emotions that she didn't know what she was supposed to do with.

So she did what she always did. She got up and got ready to face the world.

She was Kaylin.

She was strong.

Somebody had to be.

Three

Kaylin's mood improved as she started walking to school. Every step seemed to take her further away from the source of her fears – physically and emotionally.

It wasn't much of a walk, she could do it in about ten minutes if she rushed, but she always took her time. She deliberately walked slowly so she could take everything in - the perpetually dirty road signs, the dilapidated shop fronts, the little kids toddling to school with their mums and dads, the adults rushing to work. The world was full of interesting people and their life stories – you just had to take the time to notice.

Her favourite people to watch were the drivers who had stopped at traffic lights. They always acted as though nobody could see them. Kaylin would watch as they'd sing their favourite songs and tap the steering wheel, or adjust their clothes, or touch up their makeup.

People's intimate moments, displayed for all to see. A private show for their invisible audiences. That always made Kaylin smile. A glimpse of what normal people did when they thought nobody was watching.

Watching the world and observing what everybody else did each day made Kaylin feel part of society. A vicarious way to be less abnormal than she ordinarily felt.

It was also yet another reason why her timekeeping skills were not what they should have been.

Watching Kaylin walk, a bystander would be forgiven for thinking that she wasn't seeing much at all. Her eyes looking as though they were fixed on some distant point ahead, with their focus solely on that. That wasn't the case though. Thanks to exceptional peripheral vision, Kaylin noticed everything.

Even her teachers had noticed, which seemed to cause both confusion and unease amongst a couple of them.

She thought back to the previous year, and her oh-so-trendy teacher Mrs *Call me Martine, kids* Bowater. She never seemed to understand how Kaylin could read the whiteboard from the back of the room without moving her eyes. It hadn't taken long for Kaylin to pick up on the confusion, and many lessons since then had been spent stifling giggles. She'd even started to do it deliberately just to see the look on Mrs. Bowater's – *Martine's* - face.

Kaylin smiled to herself as she remembered parents' evening, and her confused teacher mentioning this to Kaylin's mum.

"She actually seems to read from the board *without moving her eyes*," she had said with a look of incredulity. "Does she do this at home?"

Kaylin had looked at her mum and an unspoken question passed between them.

How could you do this at home? Does this woman think we've got a whiteboard?!

Kaylin had bitten her lip to control what felt like it could potentially become uncontrollable laughter. She registered the restraint on her mum's face, knowing how desperately her mum would want to make a sarcastic comment.

"No, Martine," she said with a straight face, "she doesn't do that with the whiteboard at home."

Conversations with teachers always concluded the same way anyway, "Now, about Kaylin's punctuality...."

As she strolled along and got closer to school – and further from home - she felt like she could breathe a little bit easier. It felt as though she was climbing down the mountain rather than up it, so the air wasn't as thin anymore and it wasn't such a struggle to catch her breath.

Walking always made her feel better. No matter where she'd come from or where she was going, walking gave her something that nothing else ever seemed to - control.

She could choose where she went, and how fast she got there, even whether she got there at all. It was a choice. It was her choice. The only person in the world who controlled what happened next would be Kaylin. Not mum, not the school, not anybody else.

She knew that she was never really totally free while walking - eventually she'd still have to go to school, or go home, or wherever else she was expected at a certain time, but it gave her the feeling of freedom. And, in the moment that an emotion is felt, whether it's actually true or not makes no difference.

And Kaylin knew all about intense emotions. She thought back to an episode a few months earlier where her mum had tried to explain her philosophy on life. She'd noisily stumbled into Kaylin's room in the middle of the night and slammed herself down on the end of the bed, almost bouncing off in the process. The pungent stench of alcohol had surrounded her like an aura. She'd shaken Kaylin's shoulder a couple of times and stage-whispered a "Wake up!" Kaylin had been awake anyway, but turned to face her mum and asked, "what is it mum?"

Kimberley had leaned down to her only daughter's face, clearly struggling to focus eyes that had been seemingly marinated in booze.

She imparted her wisdom.

"Always go for your dreams, Kaylin," she slurred. "Make your own path in life and don't be put off by anyone."

She paused as if for effect, then held a finger up as if to underline the point she was about to make.

"Because one day it might be all you ever have."

That was the part that enraged Kaylin. The part that caused her body to flush with anger.

You don't know how right you are, Mum.

Her mum had spent her whole life following her dreams and it had got her precisely nowhere. Her dreams were literally all she had at this point. What else was there? A dilapidated flat in a shitty area with sky-high rent, and one dead-end job and soul-destroying rejection after another.

That night - and those words - had been scorched into Kaylin's brain. Like an irritating song, they burst into her mind over and over again, seemingly out of nowhere.

She even remembered the time of the conversation that night. Two forty-five a.m. Her mum had come in from a long night of 'working'. Kaylin had become accustomed to seeing her mum "going out to meet with business associates" at all hours. It was only recently that she'd understood exactly who those men were. Not because of anything her mum had said, but just because with the passage of time Kaylin had understood more about the world. Sex sells, and the pay is too much to resist for some people.

Unfortunately, Kimberley was one of them.

In the same month Kaylin had got her first period, she also started noticing the way some of the boys at school had started looking at her. She knew more about sex from the information mill that was the school playground than anything she'd been taught in class. It was just a matter of time until she'd realised the truth about her mum.

And when she did, it pained her heart more than she could have imagined.

It still did.

Then she's sitting there, after letting strangers do that to her, and telling me about dreams?! Giving me advice about how life should be lived?!

The now-familiar feeling of fire searing through her muscles returned, an almost overwhelming urge to run back home, wake her mum and scream into her face, "Where have your dreams got *you*? Where have they got *us*? *Look what you have to do so we can survive!*"

Looking back, she still didn't quite understand why she hadn't said anything that night. Maybe it was the shock of realising the truth about her mum, or the betrayal of it all. Maybe it was an overwhelming sense of sadness.

Or maybe - more simply - once again she didn't want to hurt her mum's feelings because, like it or not, she was all that she had. In fact, all either of them really had was each other. Kaylin's dad was gone. Where and why Kaylin didn't know, but he had. Her mum never spoke about him, but in her more depressed times Kaylin thought she had an idea why he left.

Maybe he couldn't take it anymore.

What if he'd seen what I'm seeing now? Maybe she did those... things with those men when she was with him...

I would've left too.

I still might.

Kaylin suddenly realised that she'd started walking faster. As though the memories were fuel, spurring her on towards...

Towards what exactly? She didn't know. In fact she was never quite sure whether she was running towards something, or away from something else.

In the end it didn't matter, she was at the in-between stage. She was walking.

Free.

Her thoughts were cut short as she heard the unmistakable sound of heavy footsteps shuffling behind her. They sounded close.

She snapped her head round sharply and her whole body tensed as if some apocalyptic battle was about to begin. A benefit of having to fight all her life was that she was always ready to fight for it in a second.

But there was nothing to fight. There was nobody behind her.

She turned slowly back around, her senses heightened for anything unusual. She began walking again, this time with her head a little higher and her back a little straighter. Her whole demeanour had changed and she was walking – as a self-defence coach might describe it – 'purposefully'.

Another noise.

Head snapped around. Muscles taut.

Nothing.

Again.

She stood staring into the empty space in mid-air where somebody should be standing. A man with a knife, an attacker, *someone*. But there was nobody.

She stared into where the eyes of the imaginary figure would be, her fists clenched and ready. Her peripheral vision saw nothing this time. No signs of people, no cats, no dogs or anything else that might have made a sound.

She realised she hadn't blinked for almost a full minute. She'd frozen completely. As ever, the hurricane was raging inside, not out.

A couple more minutes passed and she realised that the fight in her had started to drain away. She felt herself becoming less angry and more... something else. She couldn't quite place it.

She concentrated on her emotions like a patient concentrates on her body, ready to tell the doctor where it hurts.

Then it hit her.

Hope.

She was feeling *hopeful.* Two questions swirled around her head, taunting her with empty promises.

What if it's him?

What if he wants to see me?

She jerked her head, trying to shake the thoughts out, mentally kicking herself for being so pathetic.

He doesn't want to see me. And if he did he wouldn't be sneaking around, would he?

Would he...?

She paused. How would she know whether her dad would sneak around or not? They'd never even met.

She was still looking at the dead air. Visually sweeping the area for someone, something. Then the anger returned in a wave, almost knocking her over.

Someone or something made that noise. I definitely heard something.

In a second the fight came back, and Kaylin realised that now she wanted someone to be there whatever their intentions - good or bad.

In fact, especially if they were bad. At least if someone tried to attack her she could get rid of some of the aggression she'd been carrying. She'd been hoarding anger as though it was something worth hanging on to, as if one day she'd find a use for it which would justify the constant twisted feeling she felt in her stomach. Ever since her conscious mind had started working – understanding and recording her life - she'd been angry. She was at the point where she wanted a reason to let it all out and shout and break things and be aggressive. And fight to the death.

But there was no reason this time. There was nobody there. Once again the fight had risen up inside her like magma in a volcano, only to be capped before any damage was done.

Any external damage anyway.

Slowly, Kaylin turned back and started walking again. She kept alert, but there were no more unexplained noises.

She sighed.

Maybe I'm finally going crazy...

The thought was a familiar one, she often felt as though a particular moment would be the point when she'd finally slip over the edge and into the abyss.

She knew she would one day, surely it was inevitable with her life as it was, wasn't it? She'd always felt different from everybody else anyway, what difference would it make if she actually did go crazy? All she wanted was to be normal, with a normal life, and a normal family.

Instead here she was, alone. Pretending to be free.

I'm the daughter of a failed actress, and the daughter of a failed father. What exactly does that make me...?

This was a familiar thought too, it had been reverberating around inside her mind for as long as she could remember.

Kaylin kept walking, this time with her head down and shoulders slumped.

She was deep in thought. She was feeling exhausted.

And she had no idea that she was right - and that for the past few minutes, someone had been following her.

Four

"And I can't wait to see you, baby."

Adrian hung up his phone with a smile on his face.

Life was good.

He was twenty-eight years old, worked for one of the top television networks in the country, and somehow managed to have a beautiful girlfriend. On top of that, inexplicably, the sun was shining, even though he lived in London and it was nearly Christmas. Maybe global warming wasn't such a bad thing after all.

He sat outside the television network offices on a marble step, surrounded by crushed and extinguished cigarette butts. Mostly his. He wasn't one of those people who smoked because they felt stressed, he was just one of those people who liked smoking.

Now that he thought about it, he hadn't felt stressed in quite a while. In fact he'd been feeling pretty satisfied with things for quite some time, thank you very much. Ok, so the television job was just in the post room at the moment, but he'd move up. And, yeah, maybe he'd only been going out with Donna for a while but it was going well.

Really well. For once.

His friend Ian hadn't been convinced, spending almost an hour warning him that she's too attractive for him, and how that means she'll get bored first. "Pretty girls never last with normal men, Ade," he'd said with the gravity of a hundred year-old sage from some cliché-ridden film. "It'll never work."

"Cheers, Ian," he had responded. "It's always nice to get advice on women from a thirty year-old accountant whose mum still does his washing."

Adrian smiled again.

He checked his watch. Five minutes till his break was over. Should he go back in early and make a start on things, or have another cigarette?

His brain considered the question at the same time as his hand reached into his pocket on autopilot, found his packet of cigarettes, and made the decision for him. He took out his silver lighter which was emblazoned with *Mr Sexy Pants* – the remnant of a failed relationship (he couldn't remember which one) – and lit a cigarette. Specifically, the last cigarette in the pack. No matter, he'd sneak off and get more later. He only smoked twenty a day, although it used to only be ten, and before that only five. A couple of years from now, it'd probably only be fifty.

He did some mental arithmetic and worked out he'd been smoking for nine years now. Longer than most friendships he'd had – definitely longer than any romantic relationships. He remembered his first cigarette well, smoked while standing in the student union bar of the university that he'd briefly attended. It was one of those historic institutions in the heart of central London that had more pomp than it knew what to do with. He had felt destined not to last there and become one of them, and so went out of his way to fulfil that destiny.

He never officially quit, he just stopped turning up. He occasionally wondered if he was still on the books somewhere, and they were just waiting for him to get in touch so they could chase him for ten years' worth of tuition fees.

He flicked the ash from his cigarette. The only reason he'd started smoking in the first place was because of a pretty girl he thought wouldn't be interested in him because she was too attractive.

Make of that what you will, Ian...

He remembered the scene. Boy meets girl and realises girl smokes. Boy doesn't smoke, but buys cigarettes and hatches an oh-so-cunning plan. Girl walks past boy, boy stops her and asks for lighter.

Not exactly the most original opening line – "Have you got a light?" - but it worked. So did the relationship for a while. Until girl went off with other boy to be precise.

He checked his watch again. Two minutes left. He didn't want to be late back because his boss was in today, and Eugene Jones had a 'thing' about time.

On Adrian's first day, Eugene had taken him aside and warned him about timekeeping. Twice.

"I'm not a stickler or an ogre. Nothing like that. In actual fact I think I'm quite a fair manager, but I do have a thing about time."

Thirty seconds later in the same conversation, "I'm not unreasonable Adrian, but I have got a thing about good timekeeping."

Oh, well, that's a relief. As long as it's only a thing. For a minute there I thought you were being weird about it, but as long as it's just a thing then I suppose its ok. Although it does happen to be a thing that you've mentioned twice in the same conversation...

What he later discovered was that 'thing' was a euphemism for 'compulsion'.

Back in the present, he checked his watch. Time to get back.

He flicked his cigarette butt, got up off the marble step - now peppered with cigarette ash - punched his code into the door and walked back to the post room.

***

The post room was a strange place. The staff called it the dungeon, only half-jokingly too. It was in the basement, had no windows and no clocks on the wall. Just a huge room with rows of pigeonholes and piles and piles - and *piles* - of post. Letters, packages, whatever.

That morning he'd waded through the pile of smaller packages, and managed to get about halfway through. There weren't any targets to hit in this job, which he liked. It meant he could just concentrate on sorting the post while dreaming about being in one of the offices upstairs one day. It also meant he could take quite a few cigarette breaks too – as long as his boss wasn't there. With his thing.

He got his trolley and pushed it along the blood red guidance lines on the floor, passing the huge pile of 'suspicious' packages.

He'd often wondered why anybody in their right mind would leave 'suspicious' packages in their building at all. And what was the point in separating them from the other post if they're in the same room? A bomb wouldn't discriminate between different sections of the post room.

He'd also mentioned more than once that it'd be a nice gesture to move them further away from the staff at least...

He arrived at his table and started sorting through the mountain of packages in front of him. He had a good sense of what was in most of them just by the look of them. Small, square, padded envelope. CD or DVD. Either from some singer wanting to get their stuff heard or from some actor wanting to show their range. With those ones, you never knew until you opened them which senses were going to be attacked. It was like a really shit lottery.

Bigger, rectangular, padded envelope. Videotape. These had become rarer over time, but could be just as entertaining. Often they were from older singers and actors, or people who never got round to trying but wanted one last shot at the big time. Either that, or a 'hilarious' clip of someone injuring themselves for one of those 'film your relatives falling over and send it to us' shows.

Small, rectangular envelopes were a bit trickier. They generally contained audiotapes, although less people had them nowadays, so they could just as easily be diaries documenting a fan's love for their favourite TV star, or notebooks full of script ideas.

Then there were the envelopes that weren't padded but had strange bumps under the paper as though they had underwear stuffed inside.

Which they invariably did.

Adrian loved this type of package, they were always good for a laugh. Conjuring up images of a bored housewife obsessed with one of those perma-tanned, nylon-suited TV presenters, and concluding that the best way to get him to notice her would be to send a pair of knickers. Not a nice letter, not a phone number, not even a photograph. No, let's get straight to the point. Here are my knickers, you like?

Adrian had wasted more time than he would care to admit wondering whether that technique had ever actually worked. If the looks of the TV presenters were anything to go by, then no, it didn't.

Ever.

He'd nearly finished sorting through his the first batch when a package near the bottom of the pile caught his eye. It looked like one of the videotape packages, but it had thick black lettering scrawled across the front - 'Private and Confidential – I do not seek fame'. He noticed that the address itself was a bit odd too. Instead of being addressed to someone in particular – usually someone in casting, or a famous TV personality - this had 'To Anyone, Anyone who wants to see' written on it.

His curiosity piqued, he picked up the package and felt it, lightly fingering and then squeezing with both hands.

It was definitely a videotape.

But why would any of the usual bunch of wannabes write 'I do not seek fame' on it? Some kind of misguided attempt at reverse psychology? Unless it was one of the #really# crazy ones, then it didn't necessarily mean anything at all.

He flipped it over and read the spidery scrawl on the back - "Enjoy. Love you, Andy (The Artist)."

Andy the Artist? He sounds like a children's TV presenter...

Adrian flipped the package over and looked at the front again. The address was an invitation to everybody in the entire building. It didn't exactly seem like the actions of someone who didn't want fame...

Adrian knew that the wannabe stars usually found out the name of someone important and addressed their tapes to them. As if the Vice President of the company would drop everything to watch some weirdo's portrayal of Hamlet with glove puppets just because the package was addressed to him personally.

Adrian smiled. If all of Shakespeare's plays were done with glove puppets, he might actually watch some of them.

He looked again at the package, oddly drawn to it. This had to be one of the really crazy ones....

He began to feel a real compulsion to watch the tape – it seemed too good an opportunity to witness something really weird.

He looked around the busy room. Eugene wasn't here, but he was bound to come in later. He did that from time to time, probably just to see if anybody took an unauthorised break while he was awa-

No, wait a second. He's not in this afternoon. His daughter's doing that sports competition or gymnastics gala or something.

The decision was made. Adrian slipped the package under his arm, turned around and walked the fifty or so steps to the staffroom – the only place in the dungeon with a video player.

***

Unfortunately it was also the only place in the dungeon where everybody was guaranteed to be hanging around when Eugene wasn't in the building.

He walked in, and his shoulders immediately slumped as he heard an audible groan come from his lips.

Sitting on the hundred year-old, once-blue sofa were Mick *it's only a bit of fun* Granger and Margi *he's really gonna leave her for me this time* Francis.

Mick had his thick red hands on her pale bony shoulders, his sausage fingers moving in what could only very loosely be described as a massage.

They definitely hadn't planned to be there together at the same time, they definitely were not cheating on their partners with each other, and they definitely hadn't been caught together on more than one occasion in the staffroom.

They turned to Adrian, and he suddenly felt like a teacher catching a pair of his students playing truant.

"Oh hi, er, Adrian," said Mick. "Margi just had something on her, er, face. Neck. I mean neck. She had something there. On her neck."

Adrian toyed with saying, "Yeah, an overweight adulterer" but couldn't be bothered. They wouldn't get the joke anyway, then he'd have to spend three minutes explaining it.

Margi was doing her best mime of somebody with something in their eye, theatrically flicking open the mirror she kept in her bag and making a show of gently touching her eyelid. After a couple of seconds she seemed to remember it was her neck that was supposed to be the focus, so made a show of rubbing it with her hand and making loud groaning noises.

Mick must've wished he had a tape recorder.

Adrian was used to this, everybody was. But he wasn't in the mood to play along today.

"Yeah, that's... great. I hope the swelling goes down."

He gave Mick a look.

"Anyway," he continued quickly, "do you two feel like watching a tape?"

His students looked at him cautiously, then at each other, as though answering might somehow incriminate them. Margi answered first – he always thought she was the man in the relationship.

"S-sure," she said. "Why not?"

The question sounded genuine and seemed to be addressed more to Mick than Adrian.

Not that Adrian was listening. He switched on the television set – which looked about as healthy as the sofa – inserted the tape and pressed the sticky *Play* button on the front.

They were silent as the video player started whirring. It obviously hadn't been used for a while.

Snow on the screen, and nothing but static coming from the speakers.

Adrian took a seat on the collection of springs and ragged material that used to be an armchair. He wasn't concerned about the lack of picture yet, Andy T Artist wouldn't have gone to all this trouble without recording something for the entire building to watch.

An image burst onto the screen. A woman sitting on a chair.

It looked to Adrian as though she was in some kind of cell. And was she tied to that chair?

Nothing happened for a while, on or off-screen.

No static either. Just silence.

Margi frowned. "Is she dead?"

No answer.

She gave Mick a look telling him not to be so disobedient that he would dare ignore her direct question.

"I said, is she-"

The woman's eyes opened, and she blinked rapidly a few times. Her eyes said one thing only – confusion. As though she'd awoken from an unplanned nap with no idea where she was.

Her hand jerked to a halt as she tried to raise it, as though she had wanted to wipe the sleep from her eyes but hadn't realised she'd be stopped. She managed to move it a whole millimetre before realising she was securely bound to the chair.

Adrian, Mick and Margi watched as the woman – actress? wannabe? – wriggled in her restraints. The chair made strange clicking noises as it moved slightly under the woman's weight. The noise reverberated throughout the room, which Adrian now decided was definitely a cell.

They saw by her eyes at the exact moment she realised by flexing her arm and leg muscles that she was completely bound. Paralysed. Stuck to the chair, with her mouth taped up.

Then she looked straight at the camera, as though somehow looking at herself. Neither Adrian, Mick nor Margi could explain the look on her face, but later they - and the whole world - would understand it. There was an odd recognition there - a strangely horrific one - like a beautiful woman seeing her disfigured face for the first time after the accident.

It's me, but it can't be me...

Looking at the camera, she then seemed to calm for a second, almost as though the audiences' presence was helping her to cope – even though she couldn't possibly know anyone was there.

Then something changed in her eyes and they no longer said confusion. They screamed it.

Then, the voice.

"The timer starts now. You have fifteen minutes. Make it count."

Margi asked a question, a slight quiver in her voice now.

"What *is* this?"

Nobody answered, and this time Margi gave Mick no look at all. She was totally focused, as they all were, on the screen.

Adrian was studying every aspect of the scene, hoping it was fake. His unease teetered on the brink of horror as he realised there was nothing to indicate it wasn't genuine.

The only slight comfort was that he knew people did weird stuff like this all the time to get attention. Just because he hadn't seen anything that looked fake yet didn't mean it was all real.

He kept his eyes fixed on the screen, keeping his mind open that she'd done this to herself. Then, a thought.

How would she tie herself to a chair?

He thought about the logistics of it and couldn't work it out.

Then he remembered the voice. She'd obviously got her friend to tie her up, then bark things at her on screen. Maybe he was the director, or writer, or another actor who might turn up for the second act? There were a million possibilities.

He probably would've been more convinced if he wasn't trembling. And if he'd looked around at exactly that moment he would have seen Margi and Mick, their eyes burning through the screen. And if he'd seen their faces he would've known exactly what they thought about this too. It was real.

Too real.

They watched as the young woman writhed and tensed her body, straining against her bonds. Blood was trickling from her wrist where the restraints were cutting into her.

Margi gasped and covered her mouth with her hands. Mick was biting the nails off his.

Adrian's eyes danced around the scene, desperately scanning every detail of the image for any indication that it wasn't real. So far he couldn't find any. But this couldn't possibly be real. Why would someone film their own crime? People don't do this kind of stuff to each other.

But he knew they did.

They watched as the tears began running down the young woman's face, and watched as chest rise and fall in desperate bursts as her breathing became faster and shallower. Along with the clicking of the chair was another noise now – frantic grunts echoing around the cell as the woman snapped her head back and tried in vain to use her bodyweight to knock the chair over.

Then came something new, a screeching noise like an old bolt sliding open or closed. Then a similar noise, not quite the same but definitely metal sliding on metal.

Then came the climax.

To the trio watching it was unclear what came first, the sound of an explosion reverberating off the walls, or the sight of the young woman's head jerking sideways as half of her face was torn off by some invisible force.

Not that it mattered.

Margi was vomiting all over the carpet.

Mick was on his phone dialling for the police with trembling fingers.

And Adrian wished he hadn't just smoked his last cigarette.

Five

Fifty-two miles away from Adrian, Mick and Margi is another basement.

Another dungeon.

Two rooms have been constructed here, and both are shrouded in all but total darkness.

In the first one – the one which could loosely be called the office – a figure sits at a computer. The floor is cold, hard cement, the walls bare brick and looking as though they've been in need of repair for some time.

The wooden chair the figure is sitting on creaks every so often, as if even the inanimate objects in this space are screaming for mercy. The figure either does not care or has not noticed.

The light from the screen keeps total darkness at bay. But only just.

Right hand fixed to the mouse, rapidly moving back and forth, intermittently clicking like a clock gone insane.

There is the faint sound of Rhapsody In Blue by George Gershwin playing from an unknown source.

No other sounds.

No other light.

To the left of the desk, the top half of the wall is a huge sheet of glass, although what lies behind is concealed by the darkness. Whatever it is must be of some importance to the seated figure, because a camera is pointed directly at it.

Sitting next to the computer on the desk is what looks like a child's alarm clock. A yellow, egg-shaped lump of plastic with a purple face. On the top of it sits a miniature plastic fried egg, which is used to stop the alarm when it rings.

Hand moving mouse, eyes searching the screen as though some dark secret lies within.

Where are you?

The other room is going to be very famous. Soon.

The far right wall is spattered with blood, as is the floor, as is the ceiling. There is a smear leading from the centre of the room to the heavy iron door. Evidence that something - someone? - has been dragged outside.

In the centre, above the smear, sits a chair. This too is covered in blood and an assortment of other fluids. The sad details of this grimy chair and it's covering - traces of sweat and urine will be found - will eventually be known. First to the police, then to the media, then broadcast all over the world.

Just as the seated figure next door wants it.

The only clean part of this room is the mirror. A huge, spotless looking-glass almost covering the entire top half of the wall.

This room is pitch black, the only light being the unnatural glow emanating from the computer screen in the room next door. If a person were to press their face onto the glass and cup their hands around their eyes, they would clearly see that this is a one-way mirror.

Although so far there had been only one visitor to this room, and she had other, more immediate, concerns.

An office, a blood spattered cell - this is where Andy works.

Or, to be more precise, Andy the Artist - a self-given name and the only one The Artist will respond to anymore.

And pretty soon the only one the newspapers will use in their headlines to help them sell more copies to the masses.

I am Andy. I am an Artist.

I am The Artist.

Sitting here at the desk, searching through page after page of internet sites, studying posts on chat rooms. It's all here. Online CVs, biographies, and all the information from social media that a person could want to prepare for the hunt. Personality information, location information, what the person likes and dislikes. You could piece together an entire life without leaving the computer screen.

If you were so inclined.

And The Artist is more inclined than anyone.

Looking, scouring, hunting.

Where are you?

Image after image flash onto the screen. A thousand photos with a thousand names and contact details sitting next to them. Each photo posed in a studio somewhere by young actors and actresses, eager for fame. Desperate for it. Spending hundreds, maybe thousands, on it.

I'll make you famous.

Famous for fifteen minutes.

That's what you want isn't it? What we are all entitled to, isn't it?

Hand, moving. Mouse, clicking. Eyes, focused.

Where are you?

Hand moving faster, agitated. Eyes scanning, but quicker now. Desperate. A drug addict getting the next fix ready.

Looking, scouring, hunting.

Then, everything stops.

A sharp intake of breath.

Is this you?

On the screen is a picture of an attractive young girl. The Artist studies her, clicking every link and opening the various online sites one window after another. Each one providing more pieces of the jigsaw.

Eyes penetrating, burning through the screen. Envisioning the girl's future, her fate.

Jessica... twenty-four... hair, brown... eyes, green... five foot seven... trained in London... four student films... voiceover work... some modelling... contact details below...

The Artist smiles.

The strong right hand that has so far been fixed to the mouse finally releases its grip and moves to the phone. Eyes on the screen, fingers dialling.

I'll make you famous...

The Artist has found her.

The main part for Act Two.

Six

Kaylin was walking again, although this wasn't one of her preferred journeys - she was on her way home from school.

In two minutes she'd reach the alleyway near her house, which was the exact point that in recent months her stomach had begun to tense. Her guts would twist impossibly into themselves, churning and squeezing the stomach acid up until it burned her throat. For some reason, this specific point in the journey was when the reality of having to go home would hit her – and the anxiety about just what she might be walking into this time.

She supposed she could've taken the long way round to add some more time to the journey, but dismissed the thought almost as quickly as it had occurred to her. Why prolong an uncomfortable journey? She had to go home sometime, a few more minutes wouldn't make a difference.

This was the only journey that made her feel less – not more - free.

It made her want to cry that her walks home had become polluted by a sense of fear and dread. Her home had always been her haven, the place she went to that was safe from the outside world. Not anymore. Her childlike ignorance was fading fast, and she'd begun to see things for what they were, not what she was *told* they were. As she got older she understood more about what adults do, and say, and mean – and how those things are not always the same.

She had begun to understand ulterior motives and the millions ways that people pretend things to each other. A child sees a smile, an adult sees the pain behind it.

And Kaylin was very quickly becoming an adult.

As strange as it was, and as uncomfortable as she felt walking home, she often wondered if this was perversely going to be the best part. Maybe that part of life before something is discovered is the best place to be, because at least then people can delude themselves that things might be okay.

Rather than knowing they're not.

Surely it's better to think you might live than to know you're about to die?

She hated feeling like this. It was that old cliché – fear of the unknown.

What mood would is mum going to be in today? A good one? A bad one?

Is she going to be laughing and joking, or ranting and railing against the world?

The disorientation often felt too much. Knowing you're walking into a war zone is one thing – you can mentally prepare. But not knowing what you're about to walk into is its own special form of torture.

Although if recent days were anything to go by, her mother's moods was more likely to be bad than good.

There'd been entire evening meals where the main course had been served with an horrific tension on the side, and a big steaming bowl of misery for dessert.

She came out of the alleyway and walked quickly to the flat. The front door seemed imposing today, almost daring her to enter. She inhaled deeply to calm both her nerves and her stomach, and rang the doorbell.

She waited, trying to remain neutral. Trying to be ready for whatever might come.

Then, footsteps. Hard, stomping ones, each thump twisting the knot in her guts ever tighter.

The door was yanked open so fast that Kaylin felt a gust of air rush past.

Kimberley stood in front of her, she was wearing her 'nice' clothes so Kaylin knew she must have just come back from an audition.

A good audition, or a bad one?

"Why didn't you use your key? What's the point in you having a key if you don't use it, Kaylin? What's the point?"

A bad one.

In fact it must have been a terrible one - Kaylin could smell alcohol on her mum and she wasn't even standing that close. She only drank after the *really* bad auditions. And she'd started drinking a lot.

"What if I was busy? What if I was out?"

The last two questions – as rhetorical as the first batch - were fired at Kaylin from the back of her mum's head as she stomped away. Kaylin didn't bother attempting an answer. Why would she? None of the answers would have been the correct ones.

Kimberley disappeared and Kaylin assumed she'd got to her bedroom to continue the tantrum there. A child just told she wasn't allowed to go on a trip.

Kaylin stepped inside the flat and closed the door. Another deep breath, another temporary release from the vice-like grip her anxiety had on her stomach. She walked to her mum's bedroom.

She found Kimberley stomping her feet as she moved around the bedroom, as if trying to trample the carpet into the floorboards. The great Kimberley Bellos, destined to be the world's greatest living actress, having a tantrum and sulking about nothing in particular.

Maybe she was an actress after all.

She stopped mid stomp and started getting undressed.

Kaylin tried to keep herself calm. She was accustomed to her mum's random outbursts, but that didn't mean she'd become immune to them. She sighed and started trying to piece together what had happened.

She must have just got home because she's still wearing her audition clothes. The audition must have been really bad because she's been drinking. I'm going to get shouted aga-

"I just came in Kaylin. Would it be too much trouble for you to use your key so I can get changed? Would it?"

"Sorry..."

"Sorry?! Sorry isn't good enough Kaylin! Everyone's sorry but what good does that do anybody?! I'm sorry I went to that bloody audition today but so what?! I've got a lot to do. You never understand that. I have to get ready!"

"Get ready for what?"

Kimberley thrust her arms up in the air.

"Get ready for what?!" she screamed as though the answer was clear to the invisible crowd she was playing to. "To work tonight that's what!"

"Where are you working?"

Her mum froze.

Her face took on the features of a criminal who'd been so busy shouting that she'd said too much to the police. Kaylin saw the realisation written all over her face, as though her mum had forgotten the effects of excess alcohol – namely becoming as careless with words as she was with money.

"Not.... work... I... Someone's coming round and he owes me some money so I have to get ready to see him. It's for that film I told you about, the one in France. Remember?"

At this, she attempted to resume rushing around the bedroom and getting changed, allowing the nonsensical 'explanation' she'd just given to hang awkwardly in the air between them.

Trying to rush around didn't work to change the subject, and Kimberley just became a strange parody of a busy person. Moving things back and forth, looking for invisible objects. Putting on a show.

Acting.

Kaylin didn't say anything. She knew what her mum would be doing tonight. And she was pretty sure her mum knew that her only daughter wasn't stupid enough to believe the line about seeing someone who owed her money.

Who auditions someone for a film and then comes to their house to give them money? Does she think I'm an actual idiot?

She knew what this meant too, and what her mum was going to say next. She didn't need to ask, and didn't need to prompt. In fact, she didn't even want to hear it this time.

"Ok mum, I'll pack a bag and stay over at someone's house..."

Her mum froze again. She was holding a blouse, which suddenly she couldn't seem to stop looking at. Without making eye contact with her daughter, some barely audible words tumbled from her mouth.

"Alright Kay."

This was one of those times where Kaylin the Adult was understanding what Kaylin the Child never could. When she was little, she would do what she was asked and be so excited about sleeping at a friend's house that she wouldn't wonder why her mum wanted her out of the way.

But now she understood so much more.

She could read peoples' faces, and recognised what their reactions gave away. She could match these up with certain emotions, and often knew more about other people than they knew about themselves.

She knew, for example, that her mum froze the first time because she'd been caught.

Simple.

Kaylin also felt a slight twinge of something else, although she wasn't sure exactly what it was or why she'd felt it. She would later remember the 'what' as feeling like excitement, although would never be able to work out the 'why'.

Kaylin knew that the second time her mum froze had been completely different. This time it was sadness, not fear. She could see that her mum had just realised how familiar this had all become to her daughter. She didn't even need to ask Kaylin to leave the house, so accustomed was she to leaving when her mum mentioned that 'someone' was coming round for 'something'.

To spare the embarrassment of them both, Kaylin left the room.

A couple of steps later she heard her mum sigh. One of those staccato exhalations people make when they've either just finished crying or are trying hard not to.

Kaylin couldn't be bothered for tears anymore. She'd spent a long time crying and it hadn't changed anything so far in her life. What would be the point now?

She went into her room and changed out of her uniform, all the while pretending not to hear the pathetic weeping coming from the next room.

Seven

It's a commonly held belief that you can judge a person's character by looking at their friends. By studying the people that a given person associates with - their likes and dislikes, how they respond to other people, how they deal with stress – you can get a pretty clear picture of the person themselves.

Not that it works all the time. In fact, sometimes there seems to be nothing at all that two friends have in common, yet they love each other like siblings.

Kaylin and Annika had met each other nine years ago and become immediately inseparable. In the years that followed they became closer to each other than to anybody else in the world. For someone over the age of thirty, nine years might not seem a substantial part of their life. But to a fourteen-year-old girl, nine years is her entire life. As far as Kay and Anni were concerned, they were sisters. Just very different ones.

Annika's mum was a teacher, her dad a psychiatrist. Kaylin's mum was an – unemployed - actress, and as for her dad... who knew what, or even where, he was?

Annika thought she'd got life worked out – as much as a fourteen year old can anyway – but was actually quite naïve. Kaylin felt like she knew and understood nothing, although in truth she knew more about life than most of her teachers.

Annika was loud, Kaylin was quiet. The result of this was one of the few things that the two girls had in common – they both kept people at arm's length. But for different reasons, and for reasons that neither of them consciously understood.

Annika kept her distance so that nobody would realise how weak she really was. Kaylin kept her distance so as to prevent her raging emotions spilling out from the tightly-controlled confines of her mind and into her reality.

Annika's dad had noticed this some time ago. Kaylin was staying over yet again and they were all watching a comedy show on television, sitting together as a family. It was an experience completely alien to Kaylin, although also completely welcome.

Ironically, it was the happy times like that which stung her the most. That was what she wanted her life to be, what she wished and yearned for more than anything. And yet sitting there and actually experiencing it was hollow – because it wasn't *her* family.

It always felt like a tease to her, and the happiness at belonging was always tinged with sadness. And, ultimately, anger.

It was this that Annika's father had noticed.

He'd been close to falling asleep in his chair, having been up since five that day, and it'd been one of those days where the patients had drained him. Most days were fine, but then there were days when, instead of him bringing the patients up, they dragged him down. His wife always told him he needed to switch off when he got home, or he'd give himself a heart attack. Or be the next patient in need of a psychiatrist.

Sitting in his armchair, he could see his daughter's young friend from the corner of his eye. She was smiling and laughing at the television show, but there was something slightly beneath the surface which seemed to be breaking through. It was as though she was laughing *in spite of* something.

He knew about her mum's problems with keeping a job of course, and how difficult things were for Kaylin. It was lose-lose for the young girl. If her mum was sad, Kaylin was sad. If her mum was happy, Kaylin was still sad just in case her mum's happiness didn't last.

He wondered if that's what he was seeing - a girl so beaten down by life that she couldn't allow herself to be happy, because inevitably the emotion wouldn't last. Maybe for the rest of her life happiness would never be pure, but would always be tainted by a slight anger or melancholy, or...

Or maybe he was thinking too much and she'd just had a bad day at school.

He'd been ready to disregard it all as the result of his tired brain and overactive imagination – although this is never easy when the subconscious mind picks up on something negative – but then he noticed her hands.

Every so often one of her hands would close into a fist and tense until the knuckles turned white, as though some enemy had appeared that Kaylin had to be ready to fight. He watched her from the corner of his eye, wondering about the juxtaposition of a laughing young girl sitting with her best friend in a warm house, with a fist clenched so tight she might draw blood.

He watched her until the television show finished, studying her and trying to work out what was wrong, and how - *if* - he could help. He had a horrible, nagging feeling that he couldn't.

And that maybe nobody else could either.

He didn't sleep much that night, thinking about that little girl – his daughter's age – and all the problems in her life.

Kaylin didn't sleep much that night either, for the same reason.

***

Annika loved Kaylin, and Kaylin loved her right back. Staying at Annika's house was one of the few things Kaylin truly enjoyed in her life, conflicted emotions or not.

Besides, Annika's parents were always welcoming and kind to her, it wasn't their fault they reminded her of all she didn't have at home. Kaylin may have been growing up and understanding the world quicker than others - including Annika - but she was still naïve enough to not entirely recognise the pity of others. Annika's mum was often just a bit too nice to the little girl, treating her like she might break. She'd spoken to her husband about Kaylin many times, especially after the fist clenching incident when, for the very first time, he'd instigated the conversation about Kaylin.

Even if Kaylin had thought she was being pitied, she wouldn't have cared. Annika's family were how she wanted her life to be, and she felt more at home there than she did in the flat she shared with her mum. They could pity her all they wanted, as long as she felt welcome there.

Kaylin thought about her mum as she walked to Annika's house. Her mum had finally stopped crying just before Kaylin left the house, which had only been around thirty minutes since she'd got home from school. She'd become very efficient at packing her bag, although getting her things together to stay over always took less time than packing to come back. Funny how slowly people do things they don't want to do.

Annika didn't live too far from Kaylin, although the area she lived in was much nicer. She lived in a house rather than a flat, which was yet another bitter-sweet fact for Kaylin.

It was a large, detached house, with ornaments cheerfully sitting on the windowsills inside, and pot plants decorating the gravel drive outside. It was the kind of place where the neighbours spoke to each other in the street because they wanted to, not because it'd be socially awkward if they didn't. A rare situation in London by anybody's standards.

As soon as Kaylin had walked up the drive and arrived at the front door, a beaming Annika flung it open, as she always did. She'd been waiting at the window for her friend, again, as she always did. She stood in the doorway, her eyes wide and mouth open. She always looked happy when Kaylin came to stay, but she looked positively manic today.

"Guess what Kay?! And I'm not telling you like I always do cos you don't play the game cos I want you to play the game today so guess!"

"What?"

She rolled her eyes.

"Kay! Guess!"

"Um... did you get a new TV?"

"Nope. Guess again."

"I don't know... what's it about?"

"I can't tell you cos then you'll know."

"I thought you wanted me to know?!"

"No, I want you to guess!"

"Why?"

"Cos its fun!"

Annika was bouncing around like an excited puppy.

"It's not fun!" Kaylin said playfully.

"Well it's not now 'cos you're not guessing!"

"I *did* guess!"

"What, TV? That was rubbish!"

"Just tell me, Anni! You know I'm not good at this. I'll guess a few things and you'll say 'no, that's rubbish Kay, come on think!', then you'll tell me the answer anyway because it's so frustrating playing this game with me! You might as well just tell me."

"We're having Chinese food!"

Now *this* was good news. One of the very few things the girls actually had in common was a love of Chinese food.

Kaylin's face broke out into a huge smile. It'd been so long since she'd smiled sincerely she thought she might have forgotten how.

"Are we really?!"

"Yes! My dad phoned and he's coming early from work so my mum said he should get takeaway so he said what did I want and I said Chinese cos you're coming too and we both like Chinese so that's what he's getting!"

The two girls couldn't contain their excitement. They - literally - jumped up and down, loudly naming Chinese dishes.

"Spring rolls!"

"Chicken Chow Mein!"

"Peking Duck!"

"Special Fried Ri-"

"Hello Kaylin. Aren't you coming in?"

Kaylin looked behind Annika and saw her mum, who was watching in amusement at the two animated menus standing in front of her. The girls realised they were still standing in the doorway and started laughing. The neighbours probably knew what they were eating tonight.

"Oh... yes... Sorry Mrs. Nader. We were just talking about..."

"That's ok, I heard. Come in Kaylin, it's lovely to see you."

The girls sniggered to each other as they walked under Mrs. Nader's arm which was holding the door open for them above their heads.

“Oh,” she called as they walked into the living room, “and you forgot Vegetable Chop Suey!”

Eight

The first thing Kaylin noticed when she walked into the living room was the Christmas tree. It was probably the biggest tree she'd ever seen, and she began wondering how they'd even got it through the door.

She looked around the room and took in the rest of the decorations – the cards hung up on the wall across a piece of red string, the nativity scene on the mantelpiece, the shiny oversized snowflakes hanging from the light fixtures. She loved Christmas. One day she'd have her own family and her own house, and she and the kids would decorate together, and they'd make everything look pretty like it was here. Her mum would be ok by then, so she'd come round and help too.

She'd cook the huge turkey while her husband entertained the children and her mum. His parents would be there too, and they'd all talk about what an exciting year it'd been, and how nice it'd be if it snowed.

They'd all eat too much, and watch television while complaining that there was never anything good on and how everything was all repeats. Then they'd pull crackers and play games, and be a normal family.

They would. One day.

She was sure of it.

***

Forty minutes after arriving at Annika's house, the Chinese takeaway was delivered.

Forty-nine minutes later, there was nothing left but empty boxes and two teenage girls with stomach aches.

The rest of the night was as it always was in the Nader household. A combination of television, conversations about school, complaints about work, arguments over the remote control, and jokes about Mr. Nader's ever increasing bald patch. Kaylin never joined in with those, although there had been a few times she'd had to bite her lip as she'd thought of some good ones.

One thing that was certain in the house was that everything always stopped for the evening news. Annika's parents prided themselves on the fact that their little girl knew what was going on in the world – however horrible some of it may be.

As Kaylin and Annika's stomachs struggled to digest the massive amounts of food they'd eaten, the news started up on the television and the room fell quiet.

The first item was about politics. Kaylin didn't pay much attention to it, but from what she could gather some party had just elected a new leader or something. She cared as much about politics as her mum did. And anyway, she was too busy trying to get a blob of plum sauce off her top without anybody noticing the mess she'd made. Welcoming or not, Mrs. Nader liked to keep her house clean.

The second item started up, and Kaylin's head snapped up so sharply that she hurt her neck. The newsreader was talking about a killer who was targeting actresses. The police didn't know how many he'd killed, but they were advising young actresses to be very careful...

She didn't hear many other details, as her head suddenly felt like it might explode. She picked up random keywords – *brutal, defenceless victims, stripped naked* - and saw the picture of a young woman who'd been killed. The woman looked so much like Kimberley that for a second Kaylin thought it was actually her.

Even when she saw the woman's name and knew it couldn't possibly be her mum, the residual panic remained. The adrenalin pumping through her veins and flooding her with terror.

She saw that the entire family was looking at her now, their facial expressions having gone from seeing her as a content teenager to a scared little girl in an instant.

"Can I please use..."

"Of course," said Mrs. Nader, gesturing to the hallway where they kept the downstairs phone.

Kaylin jumped up and rushed out of the room.

I have to warn her to be careful.

In a calmer moment she might have realised that there was no real need for the phone call. What exactly was she going to warn her mum about? She was at the flat not at an audition, what exactly was going to happen there?

Kaylin dialled the number and bit her lip.

The phone rang. And rang again. And again.

With each new ring the mental images in Kaylin's head became more sick and depraved. Her mum *stripped naked* and being tortured in *brutal* ways, the killer laughing as he stood over his *defenceless victim.*

Kaylin fought to keep her rising panic at bay. She couldn't stop it, but she'd become proficient at preventing it from causing her to act irrationally.

More ringing.

No answer.

Come on, come on...

A sudden wave of fear swept into Kaylin, mixing with the adrenalin to cause a toxic cocktail. Maybe she had been right to rush to the phone after all. Maybe she was too late, and her mum was already the killer's next victi-

"Hello?"

"Mum? It's me. Are you ok?"

She could hear a muffled male voice saying something in the background, then her mum's best fake laugh screeching down the line.

"Of course I do Jimmy, just one second..." she said in a tone Kaylin assumed was meant to be husky. Then, in a much more clipped tone, "What did you say Kaylin?"

"Are you ok?"

Her mother's voice dropped to a whisper.

"Yes! You know I'm busy tonight, Kay. I can't talk."

"But I saw on the news that there's a man attacking actresses and killing them."

The muffled male voice made some unintelligible protestation.

Then another muffled voice, this time female. Kaylin's mum, talking to the man.

"Mum?"

No answer.

"MUM?"

"YES! Look, Kaylin I'm busy. I can't talk. Ask Annika's parents, ok. Bye."

The sound of the dial tone emanated from the earpiece like a flatline.

Kaylin noticed Annika in her peripheral vision, standing in the doorway. An expert at concealment by now, she kept talking.

"Ok then, mum... Yeah, I was just checking... I love you too... bye."

She hung up the phone and turned to Annika, feigning surprise as if she hadn't known she was standing in the doorway.

"Yeah, she's ok."

Kaylin noticed Annika's shoulders relax slightly. She wasn't good with serious stuff like this and Kaylin bet she was glad the tense – albeit small - scene was over.

They walked into the front room.

"Is everything alright, Kaylin?" Mrs. Nader asked.

"Yes, thank you Mrs. Nader. I just wanted to check. Sorry for scaring everyone."

"Not at all. I'm just glad your mum's alright."

Annika's parents shared a look as Kaylin sat back down.

Later that night, Mr. Nader noticed Kaylin's hand clenching into a fist again - opening and closing almost independently of its owner. He had special cause to be keeping an eye on his daughter's friend today.

And what a day it had been...

Even later that night, Kaylin cried herself to sleep as quietly as she could so as not to wake Annika.

Even in the safety of this home, in the warmth of the bed she shared with her best friend, she had to hide her feelings.

Even her lowest moments, it seemed, had to be hidden.

Nine

The Artist walks down Oxford Street, ready to meet the star of Act Two.

Yet another street full of people trying to look busier than they are, so they can look more important than they are, so they can feel like more than they are.

You don't fool me for a second...

It was always a source of great amusement to Andy, walking amongst these people. These people who are all too self-absorbed to notice life around them, or to pause their unnecessarily busy lives and merely take time to think for a moment, or even to notice someone who might one day end their life.

And definitely too self-absorbed to notice The Artist in their midst.

Although, maybe one day, if one of them is lucky enough to audition for me...

The Artist smiles, and is rudely brought back to reality by a shoulder barge coming from the left. A man in a suit, speaking loudly on his phone. Andy stares at him as he barges his way through everybody else too.

The familiar rage rises up but is quickly repressed.

Let it go. We've got an appointment to keep.

Andy watches as everybody else imitates the man in the suit, pushing and shoving each other as though their destination were the most important. There are always a few people who haven't been to a large city before; they're usually the ones who notice when someone barges into them. Everybody else just keeps walking.

Andy the Artist smiles at the scene – a million people passing each other without a second though. One human being barging into another without a hint of apology or recognition, looking at their mobile phones - "I'm important, people need to be able to contact me at all times!" – and eating takeaway sandwiches as they rush - "I'm too busy to make my own!" All of them using an array of tricks and techniques designed to fool each other – and themselves - into thinking their lives are important.

Being important. Being famous. Two sides of the same coin.

I can make you famous...

The Christmas lights had been switched on a few days earlier. The band of the month had turned up and were greeted by screams and shouts of "We love you!" from the masses. Women acting like girls lusting after boys pretending to be men.

And men jealous of five boys who'll one day look back and wonder why they weren't allowed a childhood.

And for what? So some rich old man, some executive manipulating them from behind the scenes can buy another yacht?

The Artist spits on the pavement. Nobody notices.

The *masses*. They love all that shit. They lap up every second of it.

Someone once wrote that religion is opium to the masses. That would make fame nothing short of crack.

In the midst of this anger Andy allows a positive thought to break through.

The lights look nice. Pretty.

Contrary to what some of the more reactionary television news presenters would soon conclude, Andy the Artist is not heartless. And Christmas in London always induced a certain indescribable emotion within that heart. Not quite happiness, not quite regret, nor sadness at not having more memorable Christmases either. The emotion was somewhere between excitement and melancholy. Excitement at all the presents and family meals and fun – for #other# people - and melancholy at the exclusivity of those things only for those other people.

Nobody would be visiting The Artist this Christmas. There was no family left to visit anyway.

Andy's pace quickens.

There was a clock over the road, lit up as part of the Christmas decorations.

One-twenty.

Nearly there.

The girl said she'd be at the café at one-thirty. She would probably be there earlier. Andy knew she was probably there right now - rehearsing what to say, how to act, the best way to sell herself, all the techniques learned from various drama schools and courses.

Andy imagined the teacher – inevitably a failed actor themselves – standing at the front of the class with an arrogant demeanour that says that he or she isn't famous because they don't want to be. Not because nobody will hire them, but because they don't want to 'sell out'. Too much integrity, too committed to the craft, dear boy.

They'd be explaining their theory of getting the job. Their gullible class lapping it up and paying for the privilege. Andy knew the patter well.

"Make them want you for this part. You've gotta go in there like you own it, like you can do the job better than anyone else. If you're auditioning to be a cowboy, turn up in a cowboy hat. If they want you to play homeless, turn up in the worst clothes you can find. *Be* what they want you to be. Play the game, you gotta play the game. Your business is you, so you gotta sell yourselves."

Once again, Andy spits.

And once again, nobody notices.

***

Three minutes later, Andy walks into the café. Yet another coffee house in central London, as if more were needed. American spellings of Italian words, and jazz music pumped from speakers hidden behind the 'art' on the walls.

The Artist always considered coffee to be something of a deception. As though the hordes of people carrying takeaway coffee cups were doing so not because they were thirsty, but in order to give the impression of a hectic life. There was the usual queue at the counter, and the obligatory

Help Wanted sign disguised as a joke - "Now you can tell everyone you're a big city barista!"

The Artist stands at the door and scans the room.

Where are you?

The excitement of the last girl was coming back. Susie. Susie the Actress who met Andy the Artist, without whom her name would probably never have been in the papers and on television.

She probably had a different type of fame in mind but...it's all exposure, isn't it? Just another part of the game, no?

The thrill was coming back now too. It was almost sexual. The illicit thrill of teaching these people a lesson, of making the industry confront something about itself. It was justice. Revenge for all of the things done in the name of *Fame.*

And fame is what they all want, isn't it? Why they do this to themselves?

Eyes scanning the room. Slowly and purposefully though, not quickly. With the relaxed air of a producer who doesn't *need* to meet with anyone.

But underneath, Andy was the same as always. Looking, scouring, hunting.

Be cool and calm. Let her see how important we are. We don't get nervous because we don't need to be.

Where are you?

Where are you, Susie?

A stab of panic.

Shit, no. Susie was the last one.

For the first time in years, the Artist feels raw panic take hold - along with the vast, conflicting emotions that had always been associated with it.

What's this one's name?

Scanning memory, mentally running through lists of names.

Come on, come one! What's her name?

This is not being cool or calm is it?

Twenty-four years old. From north England somewhere. Actress and model. Some extra work too.

What is her fucking name?!

We haven't come this far to fail now.

Then -

Jessica. Jessica?

A wave of relief washes over Andy.

Yes. Jessica. That's it.

Be calm. Relax. Her name is Jessica.

We're in a café. We're important. We are not nervous because we do not need to be. We are here to meet with a client. That's all. We are interested in her work. She is trying to impress us, not the other way round.

Jessica. Twenty-four. North England.

As if a floodgate had been opened, the rest of the details come through now.

Jessica Mahler was a young actress from Liverpool. She had trained in London at Webber Douglas, and had been in a couple of short films since then. She'd mainly done theatre work.

A typical story – good looking girl, does a bit of modelling, someone says she should be an actress, so she decides to move to London. Why wouldn't she? The streets are paved with gold down there.

Then she wastes ten years of her life doing shitty plays and working shitty jobs, living in a shitty place and probably neglecting her kid and her husband.

Her kid and her husband.

Anger tears up through Andy's soul like a serrated blade, lacerating and shredding as it ascends.

Shake it off. Forget this now, it is not helpful.

Where is she?

Now the Artist does not scan the room, but only pretends to. This was part of the act, appearing to be constantly on the lookout for the next hot young thing.

There is no real need to scan the room at all, The Artist's peripheral vision is picking up everything. And even it hadn't been, there was no doubt Jessica would be here. She'd been boasting about it on social media for the past hour...

There you are.

In the corner of the café sits the star of Act Two.

Andy notes that she looks natural, but in a posed way, as though she's rehearsed the best way to sit on a chair, the most flattering way to drink coffee. Her clothes are typically 'artistic' – *a euphemism for black and tatty* – and her hair is tied back.

The hairstyle was probably done so as not to detract the viewer's attention from her face with wavy hair or complicated styles. Textbook headshot advice given to all young actresses – no big hair, no hats, no hands touching the face.

Oh, you are an actress alright. I can smell it.

Andy, immersed in the role of the important producer, walks up to her.

"Jessica?"

"Yes?"

She looks up, and is the only actress Andy has seen who is genuinely prettier than her headshot.

"My name is Joe Cameron. We spoke on-"

"Yes, I recognise your voice!"

She stands up – big false grin, hand offered to be shaken.

Andy shakes her hand, noticing how soft the skin is. A slight thrill travels up Andy's body.

Fake laugh from Jessica. Playing the game.

"How are you, Joe?"

"I'm fine, thank you. Have you been waiting long?"

Andy sits on the chair opposite, and she takes her seat again too. The Artist watches, measuring her up as she speaks. She has an odd voice inflection, every sentence phrased as a question.

"Oh no. No, I just got here really? I had an acting class round the corner and it got kind of emotional? Y'know how it is when you're in the moment and in a scene and it's raw and you're feeling it deep down and connecting with the other actors. It just takes over and everything? So I walked for a while and then came here so I just got here really?"

She's nervous. Good.

"Well it's great to meet you Jessica. Thank you so much for meeting with me today. I love the website by the way."

"Thanks". Insincere blush. Slight glance at the ground as though embarrassed.

Andy looks at the time, quickly. Just long enough to give the impression of being in a rush.

Keep her anxious. Don't let her think too much.

"So what I really wanted to talk to you about was this show. Now, as I explained on the phone, it's kind of a reality show, but not, if you know what I mean! Basically, eight actresses pretending to be members of the public, getting into all kinds of crazy situations. It's a hidden camera show, so you're working within reality but playing a character too. You basically need to be pretty impulsive and ready for anything!"

Emphasise being impulsive. Make her try to prove herself. Otherwise she won't come with us.

"Mmm-hmm," Jessica nods. A sip of coffee. A sideways look outside the window as if posing for a magazine shoot.

"Now we've already got the other seven actresses, so basically, if you're interested, we'd need to get all of you together and see you bouncing ideas off each other. You know, banter with each other and play around a bit for the camera like you've known each other for years. Just kind of wacky. You know, just doing it rather than thinking about it. How does that sound?"

"Good, yeah," she said. Then, as if realising she needs to be more enthusiastic, "No, yeah, it sounds really good. Mmm-hmm."

Big smile, maintaining eye contact, playing the game.

Pick up the energy with this one. Force her to match our excitement. She has to want to prove she is impulsive so she will come with us.

This one is easy. Take her.

Do it now.

Andy begins to get up.

"Ok, so all that's left is to get you on film with the other girls. Just a kind of screen test to see how you all get on. I've got a studio set up at my place, which is where the other girls are. I shouldn't have left them alone really, they're probably running wild but that's what we're looking for anyway! Impulsive girls, messing about and just having a laugh. Are you ready?"

"Definitely," she says, with a slight hesitation in her voice.

Andy pauses.

"I mean... look if it's not right for you then that's ok. You don't have to-"

"No, let's do it," she says, standing up. "Let's go!"

Jessica hurriedly puts on her jacket and picks up her bag. By the time she's ready to leave Andy is nearly out of the door.

So Jessica – twenty-four years old, five foot seven, graduate of the two year course at Webber Douglas drama school in London – rushes out of the door.

Andy knows that she's wondering whether she's wearing the right clothes, whether she's got enough make up on, and whether this might finally be her big break.

Too self-absorbed to notice life around her, or to pause her unnecessarily busy life and merely take time to think for a moment, or even to notice someone who might one day end her life.

And definitely, *definitely*, too self-absorbed to notice The Artist in her midst.

Ten

Bruising exacerbates. Especially on the face.

A bruise on the face makes a hard man look harder, and a soft man even softer.

What essentially amounts to blood infiltrating into tissue and fluid passing through the walls of damaged capillaries, can go from having no effect at all to causing a response akin to insanity. The difference is context.

A martial artist with a bruise may wear it as a badge of honour. The mighty gladiator returning from the blood-drenched battle, scarred but still breathing. The more analytical mind would question the skill of the fighter and the flaws in his technique that led to conceding a hit in the first place. But that's not what the bruise says. It says I am victorious, you should see what I did to the other guy...

A five year old boy on the other hand, with a bruise on his face, is about as far removed from physical prowess as possible. No connections - conscious or otherwise - between the war scar and the mighty warrior. The response is usually either pity - "who would do that to a defenceless little boy?" - or blame - "that's what you get for running around and not looking where you're going."

The physical ailment is the same – blood, tissue, capillaries. It looks the same, it might even be in the same place. But the effect is completely different.

Context.

On a scale of emotional responses, a bruise on a boxer is at the lower end, probably a one or a two. A bruise on a child, definitely ranks much higher, say, an eight or a nine.

By that scale, the swelling on Kimberley's face would be a ten.

It was a colossal, purplish-red behemoth that pulsated and throbbed with every heartbeat. And over the past few hours Kimberley's heart had been racing faster than ever.

The worst part for her was knowing how disturbed Kaylin would be. She knew exactly how Kaylin would react. She could see it in her mind as clearly as if Kaylin was standing in front of her.

She knew how much pain it would cause Kaylin when she got home from school.

After spending the night with her friend, after calling to see if her mum was alright because she'd seen something on the news that scared her.

Sorry my only child, you'll have to go and ask somebody else, Mummy doesn't care. She only cares about Jimmy.

And after Kaylin has a night like that, she gets to come home and see just what Jimmy has done to her mum's face.

Son of a bitch.

Kimberley mentally kicked herself.

Always get the money first. What did you think would happen? Always ask for it first.

Well she'd asked for it, and she'd got it too thank you very much.

She sat at her dressing table with a glass of whisky in her hand. Whisky, no ice, just like her ex-husband used to drink.

He probably still did for all she knew.

In her other hand, she held one of those little white triangles used by make-up artists. To say she was trowelling on the make-up would be inaccurate, it looked like she'd been using a spade.

She checked the time and saw that Kaylin would be back from school soon. Her heart, which was still beating rapidly, now began to sink. She put down her drink and leaned closer to the mirror.

Two new immovable images would be burned into the memories of both mother and daughter today. Kaylin would see her mum with a black eye, swollen so much it actually affected her vision. And Kimberley would see her only daughter's face as her heart broke in yet another new and painful way. Yet another reminder of her mother's failure. Very literally staring her in the face.

She could imagine Kaylin, years from now, sitting in a psychiatrist's office and explaining how affected she'd been by all this. She'd be married to a nice man, maybe she'd have children, but it would still be there. The emotional residue.

Kimberley felt it herself from her own life, why wouldn't Kaylin from hers?

She looked at herself in the mirror.

It wasn't good.

She'd used most of the makeup. Half had gone on her bruised upper cheek and eye, stinging her face like sulphuric acid. The other half had been pasted onto the lower part of her cheeks to hide the red blotches. A cruel reminder of the tears she'd shed the night before. And this morning.

Not so strong now, are you?

She sighed loudly. Not that anybody was around to hear. She was alone.

Her mind drifted back to the phone call of the previous night. She didn't have much of a clue what Kaylin had been saying – something about the television? Maybe she'd needed help. Annika's parents might have been rude to her, or nasty, or not welcoming in some way. A swell of anger rose up in Kimberley, although surprisingly it was directed at herself rather than Annika's parents and their imaginary evil.

Nasty to her? Not welcoming?! I'm the one who hung up on her and made her stay away from her own home... Yet again.

She realised that she didn't have the right to say anything to Annika's parents even if they were somehow mistreating Kaylin. What could she possibly say? "I don't like the way you've been behaving towards my daughter."

She didn't much like the way *she'd* been behaving towards her daughter either.

She allowed her head to drop forward onto the mirror of the dressing table, exhaling as though life itself was causing her to deflate. Her breath steamed up the mirror and slowly evaporated. She watched it disappear, then flicked her eyes up to her reflection before realising that she couldn't even stand to look at herself anymore.

She closed her eyes quickly as if there was some comfort in the darkness. Like a woman alone, cowering under the bedsheets and believing it'll make her invincible to whatever is making the noise outside.

The question that had been repeating in her head on a loop now came back to Kimberley.

What have I become?

She used to have a life. She used to have a little girl who looked up to her and a husband that loved her. What kind of life was this? Acting like some kind of junkie?

Everyone else she knew – or everyone else she used to know, she'd alienated just about everybody who cared – they were all married and had children, had careers, had *lives*.

Real, genuine lives. Not this pale imitation of what life should be. They weren't running around trying to impress nameless, faceless audiences, or trying to impress some stranger conducting an audition. They were going to real jobs every day, they were getting paid – regularly, and on time! - and they certainly weren't whoring themselves out to anyone.

She shuddered. Whoring. It was too appropriate.

She opened her eyes. The comforting darkness she'd escaped into had given way to disturbing mental images that she didn't want. She still couldn't look at herself, her gaze remaining firmly on the make-up sitting on top of the dressing table.

I used to have a husband...

And she used to love him too. Robert Thorpe. Six foot five, eyes of piercing blue, light brown hair and dimples that would make American television stars jealous.

They had met through a mutual friend and were immediately attracted to each other. They made a nice looking couple, both good looking, although Kimberley in more of an unconventional way. She would lay in bed with him after yet another failed audition, and he'd tell her all the great attributes she possessed. All of the things he loved about her, about Kimberley. Not Kimberley the Actress, but Kimberley the Woman. He'd stare into her deep green eyes with love radiating from his own, and list all of the amazing qualities she had. By number two she'd be feeling better, by number five she'd forgotten the audition, and by number seven the two lovers were too busy to care about lists or auditions or anything else for that matter.

The marriage lasted fourteen months, which was the same length of time they'd known each other before they got married. Normally when a marriage breaks up both parties ask themselves where it went wrong – sometimes to assign blame, sometimes to learn from the mistakes. There was no need in this case. They both knew. It was Kimberley's fault.

She was the one who cheated, if it could even be called cheating. More of a 'career move', as she called it in order to try to mitigate responsibility somehow.

Sleeping with a casting agent!

If it wasn't so painful to move her facial muscles she would've rolled her eyes at the shame of such a cliché.

Not that it even worked as a career move anyway. She remembered, days later, saying to the agent over the phone, "But you promised..."

As though his sense of decency could somehow be appealed to and he'd uphold his end of what could be loosely called their bargain.

No mitigation here though. There couldn't be when a – very - imperfect wife cheats on her – very - perfect husband with another man, then gets pregnant and doesn't know who the father is. But leads her husband to believe it's him.

And as if that wasn't enough, then came the topper. Five months into the pregnancy she told him that the child might not be his, blurting it out in the middle of an argument no less. She'd had too much to drink, and Robert had told her that she should look after herself and their unborn baby. Her reply?

"What do you care? It's probably not yours anyway."

If nothing else, the whole incident should've taught her to stay away from alcohol.

To add insult to injury, Robert had been begging Kimberley to have a child, but she always said she didn't want to because it would be the death knell of her career. As if Hollywood would soon be calling.

Abortion had never crossed her mind once she'd actually fallen pregnant - as far as she was concerned it was tantamount to murder. Robert agreed. Funny how morality works sometimes.

As far as ending a marriage went, she'd covered all bases. Lies, infidelity, deceit, and just to round things off the possibility that she was pregnant by someone else. And keeping it.

At least she was good at something, even if it was the destruction of everyone and everything she cared about.

She shook her head at the memories, momentarily forgetting about the bruise until it began to sting.

Robert had loved her more than she could believe one person could love another. She knew that must have made the pain of her betrayal even more intense. She knew what emotional pain was like, that it can be almost tangible, contracting the internal organs every time a particular song, sight or smell sparks an old memory.

Robert used to tell her that he came alive when they'd met, as if his whole life had been a prologue to their meeting. She remembered his final words, his voice dripping with hate and love and fear, "I would've forgiven you almost anything. But how could you do *this*?"

She remembered his eyes as he spoke. Those pained eyes. The love that used to radiate from them all but gone, consumed by thick cataracts of pain and hatred. Purity drowned beneath an ocean of tar. The heavy black mass suffocating the innocence beneath.

Another immovable memory, another reminder of her total failure as a human being. Etched with a rusty blade into her soul.

She knew she was wrong. And she was paying for it. Every day she was paying for it. But surely she'd paid enough now?

The sound of Kaylin's keys in the door startled her.

She had been hoping that Kaylin would use the doorbell, which would have given her some time to get composed.

She'd forgotten that the last time Kaylin used the doorbell she'd been shouted out for not using her key. It was a small mercy that she'd forgotten; Kimberley Bellos had experienced enough self-loathing for one day.

Kimberley leapt up from the dressing table and scrambled to the bedroom door, closing it just as the front door opened. There was no lock on the door but it didn't matter, Kaylin never came in when it was closed.

Kimberley stood with her back against the door - the raised drawbridge of a castle under siege.

Closing the door so her daughter wouldn't see her face. Kimberley almost laughed. It was juvenile, and not exactly a long term solution.

"Hi Mum!"

Any thought of laughter vanished.

"Um... hi," Kimberley called from behind the door. "I'm just... one minute."

She ran back to the dressing table and caught sight of herself in the mirror. She'd been so focused on hiding that for a moment she'd forgotten about her face, and nearly yelped at the disfigured stranger who was looking at her. Half of her face was a pulsating red and purple *thing*, the kind of injury that makes onlookers flinch and instinctively put their hands to their faces. As if there was some contagion in the air and they were hurting too.

She stared at herself and realised the futility of using makeup. It hid nothing.

"Mum?"

Kaylin's voice shook Kimberley out of her shock and back into her panic.

"One minute, Kay."

She started noisily picking things up and putting them down again, hoping Kaylin would assume she was busy and go to her room or watch television or something.

"Mum?"

Kimberley sensed apprehension in Kaylin's voice now.

"I'm ok sweety, I'm just doing some cleaning and things. Why don't you wait for me in a minute because I'll be out then and not busy anymore."

Kimberley began thinking about what she'd eventually say to Kaylin. She couldn't hide forever.

Eleven

"I'm ok sweety, I'm just doing some cleaning and things. Why don't you wait for me in a minute because I'll be out then and not busy anymore."

Kaylin felt something happen in her body. A strange hybrid of confusion and anger rose up inside her, forging her muscles into steel – ready for whatever was to come. Once again her subconscious mind had realised something that her conscious mind didn't yet understand.

Her mind became consumed by a suffocating panic amidst a swirl of confusion.

Her mum's voice, her tone, something was wrong.

And she'd never called anyone *Sweety* in her life...

Maybe it's another client?

She dismissed that thought as quickly as it came, her mum wouldn't have said she was cleaning, she would've said she was in a meeting or having an audition. How else would she explain the man walking out of her room later on?

No, this was something else.

Her mind flashed back to the item on the news last night, and as it did her body was assaulted by yet another shot of adrenalin. The murders. A man killing actresses in London. *Brutalising* his *defenceless victims.*

The adrenalin took over completely, and Kaylin The Warrior prepared for war. She launched herself at the door and barged it open, her muscles steel, her determination iron.

The shock in Kimberley's eyes was only matched by the burning ferocity in Kaylin's. She had opened the door ready to fight – ready to kill – anyone on the other side who was hurting her mum.

But there was only Kimberley there - shocked, bruised, and with a look of terror on her face. Kaylin looked around to find the source of her mum's fear, before realising that she herself was the source of it.

The angry inferno blazing inside Kaylin was rapidly extinguished by the torrents of sadness within, pouring down like a monsoon. She stood there open mouthed, a scaled down version of a Munch painting.

They stood and stared at each other. Mother and daughter each trying to make sense of what they had just witnessed.

The silence had become a presence all of its own in the small room, a gaping chasm relentlessly growing with each second, increasing the distance between the two people standing on either side of it.

Kimberley's face suddenly broke into a lopsided, insincere smile.

"I fell down-"

" – the stairs?" Kaylin finished, fighting back tears at the battered face she loved so much.

Kimberley smiled and threw her hands up in the air, like a little girl excited that her friend had guessed her secret.

"Yes! Such a cliché isn't it? I was walking and not looking where I was going. Um... you know me Kay! And I just, you know..."

"Fell?"

"Yes."

Kaylin's sharp eyes focused solely on her mum. She stared as if trying to scrutinise her mum's very soul. She was lying, she had to be lying, but Kaylin couldn't prove it.

Kaylin's head swam with a heady mix of emotions. Fear, confusion, anger, rage, sadness, and now... something else.

It didn't take her long to realise what it was.

Disappointment.

The stairs. Is that the best she can come up with? Does she really think I'll believe that?

She felt crushed and defeated. She could argue and try to catch her mum in a lie, asking her mum which stairs she fell down, and asking why the rest of her seems unharmed.

She could ask why, if the explanation is innocent, her mum had been hiding from her, and question aloud how much of a coincidence it was that this happened after that man came round.

But there was no point.

It'd be lies, and more lies, and more lies.

She gave up. She didn't care anymore.

She was disappointed in her mum for lying and letting somebody hurt her like that, but in a way she was more disappointed in herself. She'd snapped and was ready to fight to protect her mum. She'd wasted her energy, and for what?

Her shoulders slumped as she realised that her mum didn't need saving from other people. Anyone trying to rescue her would have to save her from herself. Yes, someone had hurt her, but she was the one who had given them the opportunity, whoever they were.

She looked again at her mum. At her beaten face, caked with makeup and smeared with tears. She wondered if her mum had applied the make up for her benefit, so that she wouldn't think anything was wrong.

Her beautiful mum, her face destroyed.

It was the most pitiful thing Kaylin would remember seeing for a long time. And she knew that it would stay with her. She knew that some images never fade, they hang around and erode you from the inside, affecting you in ways you'll never comprehend.

"Well, as long as you're ok," Kaylin said quietly.

Then, as was becoming the custom in these situations, she turned and walked out of the room.

***

Kimberley stood in her room as her daughter walked away. She'd been wrong about two new immovable images being created today.

There had been a third.

Kaylin's face when she first opened the door had been a mask of twisted rage. Her eyes were like laser-guided weapons, focused on some enemy, some foe.

For a reason she didn't understand, Kimberley's mind had flashed to her ex-husband for a second, before focusing back on Kaylin.

The only consolation was that Kaylin had seemed to relax just before she'd left the room, her shoulders seeming to lose their tension. Kimberley took this as a sign that her daughter wasn't worried anymore, in spite of the horror she'd seen on her face.

Kimberley thought of the last time they'd argued in this room, when she'd told Kaylin that someone was coming round to give her money. She suddenly felt exposed again, naked. As though Kaylin could see right through her.

And, unfortunately for both of them, she could.

Twelve

Kaylin went to her room and shut the door.

Just like her mother's door, there was no lock on this one either, but she cared as much about that as her mother had only a short while ago.

She dropped her school bag and sat on her bed. She still wouldn't allow the tears to come.

The anger she had felt had shaken her. She'd gone through a thousand emotions in the space of thirty seconds, but it was the anger she kept coming back to. She had always been protective over her mum, and was always ready to fight if she had to. But this felt different. She not only felt that she was *ready* to kill to protect, but that it was what she actually *wanted.*

Her mind flashed back to the news report on the murders. She'd kill that man if she had to, there was no doubt about that. She'd kill anyone who tried to harm her mum.

A sliver of doubt crept into her thoughts. Would she really go that far for her mum anymore?

The disappointment she'd felt only a few minutes ago was solely because of her mum. Why should she even care anymore? She was sick of trying to look out for her, worrying about her.

And why was she worrying anyway? Because of situations that #she'd# got herself into. The auditions, the 'clients', all of it. It was self-imposed. Unnecessary.

Kaylin sighed, another *very big sigh for a very small girl.* She allowed herself to go limp and fall backwards on her bed. She lay at almost a right angle, her feet still on the floor.

She thought of all the hours she'd spent in this room in this very position, staring at the ceiling and worrying about her mum.

The scene always played out the same way too. She knew exactly what came next. She'd been forced into participating in this twisted play enough times to know what order everything would happen in.

She comes home, her mum does something stupid, things get awkward, they stay in their separate rooms for a couple of hours, then come out again and act as if nothing happened.

Then it happens again in a few days, and again, and again.

She was sick of it. It was too predictable. It was getting boring.

That's when there was a knock at her door.

Kaylin sat up quickly, giving herself a slight head-rush.

"Come in?"

The phrase came out as a question, which in a way it was.

The door opened slowly, as if the wood itself wasn't sure what was about to happen and wondered whether allowing it was a good idea.

Kimberley stood in the doorway.

"Hi Kay."

Kaylin stared at her mum, confused as to how to respond. This wasn't part of the usual routine.

Her mum was standing in front of her, a lost child in strange territory.

She studied the bruise on her mum's face. She looked so weak, so small. Kaylin was enraged that someone had done this, but still couldn't shake the anger at her mum for letting it happen. She suddenly felt an overwhelming sadness, both for her mum and for herself.

Then she did something she hadn't done in front of another person in years. Her defences crashed down, and she began to cry.

The pent up tears at last finally released. The relief at allowing herself to cry was almost as overwhelming as the emotions that caused them in the first place.

Kimberley rushed over to her daughter and in one perfect maternal movement sat next to her on the bed, enveloped her in her arms and comforted her like only a parent can.

Kaylin leaned in to her mother and sobbed onto her breast. The memory of their argument and her disappointment at her mum left in an instant. None of that mattered. She was fourteen years old, she was sad, and she wanted her mummy.

Kimberley's embrace tightened around her little girl.

"It's ok, it's ok," she said as she stroked Kaylin's hair. "One day it'll be all alright Kay. I know it's hard but I'm doing this for us, for you."

Kaylin looked up at her mum.

"Your... face. Who? What happened?"

"Shhhh. It's ok. It doesn't matter, it's over now. It looks worse than it is Kay. I'm sorry I lied but I don't want you worrying about me."

Kaylin kept her head against her mum's breast and looked down at her mum's lap. She could hear her mum's heartbeat. It was nice. Comforting.

They sat like that for a long while. This time it was Kaylin who spoke first and broke the silence, continuing the conversation as though there'd been no pause at all.

"I do worry about you though, mum. When I called you, I'd seen something on the news about a man who..."

She swallowed hard so as not to start crying again.

"...who was killing women. Actresses. And I got scared and thought of that man coming to the house, and..."

She trailed off, not wanting to verbalise her fears any more than she already had done.

"Kaylin, I'm fine. I'm ok. See? I'm here aren't I? Don't worry. I'm a tough old girl! Nothing's going to happen to me."

"It already has mum. So much has."

Kimberley lifted Kaylin's face so they were looking at each other. Kaylin almost recoiled at being this close to her mum's damaged face. But she didn't. This was her mum and this was closer than they'd been for a very long time, in so many ways. Her mum spoke slowly and calmly.

"Nothing is going to happen to me," she repeated. "Ok?"

Kaylin nodded. She felt better in spite of knowing her mum couldn't guarantee anything.

Mother and daughter hugged again, tighter than before, and Kaylin smelt that familiar mix of her mum's perfume, clothes and hair. It was a breeze of cool air on the hottest day of the year, a moment of silence in the centre of a soulless metropolis. She felt better immediately. She was home again.

Then she did another thing that she hadn't done for a very long time. She asked her mum a question that she hadn't asked her for years.

When she was younger and had a bad day at school, or felt low, or even just if she felt like it, she knew that asking her mum this one question was guaranteed to cheer her up.

As her mum's hug grew even tighter around her, as though Kimberley was trying to completely envelop her daughter with love, Kaylin softly asked the question.

"Mum, what's it going to be like when you're famous?"

Kimberley loosened her hold momentarily, then tightened like a vice around her little girl. Kaylin thought she was probably touched more deeply by the fact that she had asked that question once more than by the words themselves.

Kimberley moved back slightly and looked directly into her daughter's eyes.

"Oh Kay, it's going to be amazing. We'll have a massive house with a butler! We'll go out to eat every night at all the best restaurants. All the poshest places. Chauffeur driven, of course! You'll have wonderful clothes and diamonds dripping from your ears and neck and anywhere else you want them, Kay! You'll have a beautiful car of your own too. You could have your own house if you like. Three houses! We'll go to all the big premieres and meet all the people you see on TV. And we won't worry about money ever again! Not once! We can go on holidays whenever you want and wherever you want!"

Her mum gasped, as though she'd just remembered the most important part.

"And we'll have a swimming pool and a jacuzzi! With as many bubbles as we can! We'll live somewhere hot if you like, no need to stay in England forever. And anything you want you can have, Kay. Anything. I'll give you anything."

Kaylin had forgotten how much she loved hearing her mum talk like this. It was a dream, of course, but it was her mum's dream and she loved watching her as she told it.

Her eyes lit up, and a kind of strength shone through. As though just talking about these things with determination would make them happen. As if the more she emphasised the words, then the more likely it was that all these things would come to pass.

Kaylin felt so loved when her mum was like this, it reminded her that all these things they were going through would work out. Her mum was going through all of this for them, not just herself.

Most of the time, Kaylin felt slightly sad in the knowledge that these things could very easily never happen. But not this time.

This time her mum had gone from bruised and weak to forgetting about her face and their other problems and being strong again. Kaylin wasn't about to take that away from either of them.

Kimberley was standing up now, elaborating even more on the utopian life they were going to lead, excitedly gesticulating. She was describing the clothes, the houses, the jets, the yachts, and all in minute detail.

Her mum had come alive again. Her old mum was back, not the one from last night or even from an hour ago. The mum she had when she was little. She was strong again, stronger than Kaylin, stronger than anyone.

Kimberley finished describing their new life, sat back down on the bed and hugged Kaylin again.

"Kay, it's going to be wonderful. I don't want you to worry about anything. Not about money or about me or anything. We're ok. And #everything## is going to be ok. In fact we're going to be great! Alright?"

Her little girl nodded in her arms and didn't let go. There was that smell again and Kaylin The Little Girl was fine.

Kaylin The Warrior had left, there was nothing to fight here.

Her mum held her for what felt like a few minutes but must have been at least half an hour. Kaylin felt like she was falling asleep in her mother's arms, and wanted to hold onto the feeling for as long as possible.

As the veil of sleep fell on her, she said the one thing she wanted to make sure her mum knew.

"I love you, mum," she said quietly.

"I love you too, Kaylin," she heard her mum say.

She felt her mum lay her gently on her bed, and a few seconds later heard the faint squeak of her door being closed.

Kaylin fell asleep, and Kimberley felt as though her little girl loved her again, and that maybe their life really would be ok.

Neither of them had any idea that, for the second time this week, Kaylin had been followed to school.

Thirteen

Jackie thought this might finally be the day where she'd fall asleep in the staffroom at work.

Her head lolled forward every so often, causing her reflexes to kick in and jerk it back up before she fell forward onto the floor. She looked up at the clock, and wondered if the day would ever actually end.

It was ten minutes past eleven, and time for her daily ritual.

She pushed herself up off the chair, thinking back to when it didn't take so much effort, and walked over to the grimy microwave.

She pushed the oversized #open# button and the microwave door swung towards her, presenting her with the sight of stained walls and the smell of stale food. The perfect encapsulation of the rest of the staffroom. Maybe even some of the staff.

She remembered being shown this room on her first day in the job. She looked in disbelief at the yellowed, peeling wallpaper, and wondered just what she kept stepping on that crunched underfoot. The carpet had more food in it then some restaurants.

It's not much, she'd thought, but at least it's got a microwave.

Back in the present, she opened her plastic shopping bag. The ritual was about to begin.

First, take food out of bag, then unwrap package, pierce film lid – four times, with a fork - place in microwave, full power for five minutes, let stand for one minute.

Then, sit on manky chair, eat, and try not to sigh too loudly as it might depress the cockroaches.

Then, after all that excitement, back to work.

Jackie bought exactly the same food every day. Not that it tasted particularly good, but she knew it was filling and fairly cheap.

She liked buying it on the way to work to save time on her break, not that she had anything much to do this time of the day. One day last week she got so bored that she ended up reading the packaging of her healthy eating lasagne - two hundred and fifty-five calories, nine grams of fat, ten grams of carbohydrate, and six grams of protein. Was that healthy? She honestly didn't know, but the use of the word in the title was enough to convince her to buy the thing.

It tasted mildly like pureed cheese and onion crisps, which definitely weren't healthy...

Just in case, she always ate an apple afterwards too, just to give her body that extra nutritional treat.

As the microwave started to heat her 'food', she sat back down. It'd been one of those days, although when hadn't it?

She was thirty-eight years old and had been in the same job for ten of those years – stamping and sending an assortment of items for a film company. She had essentially been a glorified post box for a full third of her life. No children, no husband. And on top of all that, she was still trying to come to terms with the fact that her parents had given her a ridiculous name.

The thought occurred to her roughly twenty times a day that every other female Jackie in the universe was a Jacqueline. But not her. Nope. That would be too normal.

Her mind drifted back to the week her father had died and her mother had been sorting through his things. It had been a swelteringly hot day and the two of them were rifling through folders, papers, receipts and all sorts of other rubbish in the spare bedroom. Sleeves rolled up and sweat rolling down their foreheads, the whole shebang. Then her mum had held up a yellowing piece of paper, so brittle it looked like it'd snap at any moment.

"This," she told her daughter, "is your birth certificate Jack."

As she took the document she clearly saw the name that she'd loathed for so many years, defiantly and mischievously staring back at her.

Jackie Mason.

They had somehow managed to name their first and only child – their first and only *female* child - after a famous male comedian. If it wasn't for years of teasing and bullying at school she probably would've seen the funny side.

She got up and pretended not to hear her knees creak, lamenting that her parents could at least have given her a middle name. Although knowing her parents they probably would've chosen Stone or Free...

She took the apple out of the shopping bag, washed it, dried it, put it on a plate. As always.

She sat down, feeling tempted to sigh again but not able to muster the requisite energy.

Her break was the first of the day, and she hated the timing of it. It meant a break from eleven till twelve, then nothing but solid work until the end of the day.

The breaks were also all done one after another, so it's not like she'd have any company either. Sixty uninterrupted minutes of lasagne, apple eating and reminiscing.

Does it get any better than this?

She sincerely hoped so.

What Jackie didn't know was that a few days from now she'd be wishing for these innocent moments again, the way a person wishes for the past after some life changing event. They romanticise what came before, and delude themselves that life was perfect back then, that things were all ok until ##that# happened.

But they weren't ok. They just weren't as bad.

Jackie sighed again, having managed to find the effort from somewhere. She looked over at the television, and something snapped.

Ok, enough Jackie! Put the television on for pity's sake! There's got to be something on to stop me wallowing in self-pity like some kind of... miseryguts in some... kind of... miseryplace.

She wasn't as good at funny lines as her namesake.

She got up - defiantly, as though somebody had been holding her down and she'd finally decided to get up and fight – and switched on the television.

Flicking through the channels, she soon realised that only five of them actually worked. Her choice was between two quiz shows, two chat shows, and a documentary about failing cat homes.

Mercifully, she didn't flick onto a channel showing with one of those 'consolidate your debts' adverts. A fading star using what fame they have left to sell loans to people who can't afford to pay the ones they already have.

Jackie smiled. So it #could# be worse.

The microwave beeped and, in an action worthy of Pavlov, Jackie salivated a little. She was starving. And she always hated to use that word because her mother always told her that she was never really starving, just very hungry. But call it what you want to – hungry, starving, peckish, whatever - she needed some food.

It was as she turned away from the television and back to the microwave that she noticed the package.

A big, padded envelope that had been cut open at one end and was lying on a small shelf near the television.

She felt drawn to it, but couldn't quite work out why. Her subconscious mind understood her curiosity perfectly though, running through a list of subliminal questions in the recesses of her mind. Why was an envelope in the staff room and not the post room? Did someone steal it? Why is it only half open? What does that writing say?

And wasn't there something on the news about a video at a television company the other day?

She walked over and looked down at it tentatively, as though it was a coiled snake that might at any moment spring up and give her a nasty bite.

And it would.

But not yet.

She angled her head round to read the message that had been written on it in thick black pen.

Private and Confidential – I do not seek fame.

Her eyes moved down to the writing underneath. *To Anyone, Anyone who wants to see.*

Her brow furrowed involuntarily. Another Pavlovian reaction.

She picked up the package to feel its weight. It was definitely a video tape. They may be getting rarer but she was old enough to remember when there was no alternative to good old VHS.

She flipped the package over, being careful not to drop the video out of the open end.

This time she read aloud.

"Enjoy. Love you, Andy (The Artist)."

She whispered the last part, as if the parentheses were a stage direction.

She suddenly wondered how the package had even ended up here.

Her mind played out various scenarios. Any one of her colleagues could have brought this in here. To be fair, even someone that didn't work here could've brought it in, security wasn't what you'd call tight in this place.

But why would they?

She slowly, cautiously put her hand inside the package - *in case the s-s-snake struck* - and pulled out the tape. All the while she wondered why someone would bring a package from the post room to the staff room, open it halfway, and then just leave it there.

In normal circumstances maybe she would've taken that as a sign that there was nothing to watch, that the video was maybe a bit boring. But something felt off. None of the scenarios in her mind quite aligned as they should have.

She began to feel uneasy and morbidly curious. And why had the word *morbidly* entered her head?

Question after question played across her mind. Who is Andy? Did they mention him on the news too? Had she even seen this on the news or was she confusing it with a film she'd watched?

She put the video into the player and picked up the remote control, still thinking about who left this package just sitting here. And why.

Maybe Paul left it as some kind of joke?

Or Lynne?

Steve!

Something flashed in her mind as a connection was made.

Yeah, that sounds about right. He's always bringing letters and rubbish in here. Why not a vid that looks a bit interesting? I bet he thought it was blue, the cheeky sod.

Jackie didn't know – and never would – how right she was. Steve was the one who had brought the video into the staff room, after swiping it from the packages pile because it looked like it might be porn. To a man like Steve, a video with 'Private and Confidential' written on it could only mean one thing. He'd had every intention of watching it, until he glanced out of the window and saw Stacy outside the building, smoking a cigarette and looking bored. To say he carried a torch for her would be like saying that the universe is pretty big. He'd dropped the package and rushed down the stairs, not knowing just what he had been holding in his hands.

Jackie's fear had dissipated now. The video was either good weird or porn weird, but shouldn't be scary weird.

She sat down and pressed play, not knowing that Act Two of The Artist's production was about to begin.

The small television screen filled with white noise, and a crude hissing noise blared from the speakers. Jackie was about to turn down the volume when a piercing alarm filled the small space, startling her and causing her to drop the remote control.

She fumbled for it, but by the time she'd retrieved it and looked back up at the television, an image burst onto the screen. One which would one day become an iconic image burned into the minds of everyone who saw it.

A solitary figure strapped to a chair and staring disbelievingly into the camera. The condemned facing the firing squad.

Jackie stared into the face of the young woman, watching as she began to realise her predicament.

Then, a voice. *That* voice. The one that the police had been analysing since the first murder. The one that experts had been listening to on a loop for sixteen hours straight. Trying to identify the accent or pitch or something under all the distortion.

Andy's voice.

"The timer starts now. You have fifteen minutes. Make it count."

Unlike Adrian, Mick and Margi – the first audience of The Artist - Jackie was in no doubt as to whether this was real or not. Maybe she hadn't truly calmed down and was still in a heightened state from finding the package in the first place, or maybe she'd realised something, some detail, about the scene unfolding on the television. Either way, she was in no doubt.

This was real.

And she had definitely seen something about this on the news.

The woman – who Jackie would later find out was named Jessica Mahler - struggled and jerked against her restraints just like Susie (Hilary and Anthony's *amazing little girl*) had before her. Jackie could see she was clearly having trouble breathing, which was no surprise given that her mouth was taped and she was bawling. A slightly congested nose isn't conducive to good respiration, but a totally congested nose and an obstructed mouth would make it almost impossible.

Jackie realised she herself was cupping her mouth with both hands.

If asked later, she wouldn't remember putting them there at all, just like she wouldn't remember furrowing her brow or salivating. Just another reflex action with no thought behind it. Pavlovian. Another natural response.

There was nothing natural about the scene on the television in this little staff room.

The girl's wrists were bleeding, and she kept giving haunted, pained looks to the camera. For one awful second Jackie would've sworn the girl was looking #through# the television. Staring her vacant, desperate stare through the electronic device and directly into Jackie.

Jackie knew that wherever the girl was staring, she was staring through time - *because surely the girl's dead now? This tape is old. This isn't happening now, this happened in the past. But when? A few days? Months? Years?*

The woman held her gaze to the camera until Jackie almost couldn't stand it anymore. She was somehow screaming through her eyes, communicating something primal.

Help. Me.

Jackie heard a screech come from her own mouth, muffled because of her cupped hands.

After every few moments of struggling, almost as if on cue the girl's eyes would flick back to the camera and burn through it. Desperation turning to something else. Anger? Yes. And was it fear too? It looked like it.

It felt like it.

Oh, please stop looking at the camera. Can you even see it? Do you even know it's there?

Eyes blazing into the camera. Relentless, pleading, horrific.

Jackie shifted in her seat, the fear close to unbearable.

Stop looking at me!

The girl's fingers were clenching and unclenching. They began twitching like a spider on a hotplate. Jerking and tensing, as if trying desperately to grasp the situation and control it.

Jackie was reading her mind.

If I can just... get one of my... hands... free...

But she couldn't.

None of them ever would.

All of a sudden the smell of Jackie's food reached her from the microwave, causing her stomach and throat to tense up. Nausea swelled and rose up inside her like expanding foam.

She fought the urge to vomit. She needed to keep watching.

What is this?

Who *is this?*

If this were a film then the soundtrack to the scene unfolding on the screen would have started slowly and quietly, with the faintest hint of a regular heartbeat in there somewhere. Then it'd get louder and louder and faster and faster. The camera would cut to a close up of the girl's legs, strapped tight to the chair. Then, her wrists and spider fingers dripping blood. And lastly her face, a perfect picture of absolute terror now. No anger left, not even fear. Pure terror. Sheer survival instinct. No thoughts, no attitudes coming through, no plan, no ideas. Just terror and survival instinct battling it out.

Jackie was crying now. Loudly.

Like the victim of some terrible tragedy in a foreign country, screaming at the camera for help. She was reading the horror in the girl's eyes, horrified at what was happening, terrified at what might happen next.

And then, it came.

The soon-to-be-familiar sound of metal sliding on metal.

The soon-to-be-studied sound - *Detective Russell, what calibre do you think this is?* - of a gunshot. No bodies will ever be discovered so the police will only have the videos to work with.

The girl's body was suddenly racked to the right of the screen, and dark blood pulsed from her neck.

Jackie's scream caught in her throat as the blood gushed out of the girl on the screen. The colour in the girl's face began to drain away as the bleeding got slower and her breathing became shallower.

Then, silence. For an eternity, silence.

The girl's head slumped forward and she was still.

Jackie could feel how tense her own body became at this point. She somehow found her voice and screamed at the screen.

"NO! She's just a girl. She's-"

She stopped as the bleeding girl jerked slightly. A slight twitch, but enough to know that...

She's still alive.

Jackie watched her head, lolling slowly from the left to the right, and the eyes struggling to focus but fixing on something, on someone. Her pupils dilated as though looking at the gun, or gunman, or whoever or whatever was in that part of the room.

Her eyes suddenly widened, seemingly pleading for mercy. There really was nothing else left.

Just pleading.

Please. I'll be good, I'll be good, I'll be good. I promise, I promise, I promise.

At the very same moment, in front of a television screen in a tiny staff room with peeling wallpaper, Jackie was saying the same things aloud to nobody.

"Please! Please! Let her go!"

Pleading with someone, some unknown body standing with a loaded gun aimed at this young girl's head. Nothing left to say. Just, please.

Please don't kill her.

Another gunshot rang out, travelling once again through time and space.

This time the aim was sharper, and the bullet hit accurately, entering the middle of the girl's right temple and exploding out of her left.

She slumped in her chair. There would be no movement now for sure.

Jackie screamed, and the image on the screen disappeared again.

White noise again.

Fourteen

Kaylin walked through the school gates and began the long journey from there to her classroom.

The corridors were quieter than usual.

No, not quieter. *Deserted.*

As if some apocalyptic virus had wiped out humanity, leaving nothing but this manmade structure as a reminder of what once was. No people, no life, just an eerie silence.

It was late too. Kaylin didn't know what time exactly, but it #felt# late.

She also felt afraid, although she had no idea why.

A voice echoed down the barren corridor, Kaylin instantly recognising it.

Annika.

"Come and see what I've found Kay!" Annika called out. "You won't believe it!"

For some reason her friend's voice caused a shudder through Kaylin, as though there were some ominous warning in those words.

Outside of her dream, lying safely in her bedroom, Kaylin's brow furrowed slightly. One of those sleeping gestures that nobody ever knows happened. Just another hidden movement that nobody will ever see.

Back in the dream, Kaylin felt her anxiety ratchet up a notch.

"Where are you?" Kaylin cried.

Kaylin heard a muffled response, sounding like Annika's voice but possibly belonging to someone else. Her ears were confused by the words being skewed and distorted as they ricocheted off the walls.

Her eyes scanned the corridor, frantically trying to locate the source of the sound.

The sounds quickly turned into uncomfortable moans. Then from uncomfortable moans into scared shouts, which got louder and more desperate with each passing second.

Kaylin began running all over the school, taking the stairs two steps at a time as she bolted down each corridor. Opening doors, scanning the rooms, then closing them again and rushing to the next one.

She was ready to protect Annika, or her mum, or anyone else that needed protection.

Ready to kill.

She was the strong one, she had to be. She'd help. She'd find Annika and she'd make them pay. Whoever ##they# were.

Getting to the top of the school where the corridors snaked around and in on themselves, she navigated her way to the science laboratories that she'd sat in a thousand times. There was something different in the air today. An invisible fog, an ominous warning.

She heard Annika's muffled screams again.

"Where *are* you, Anni?" Kaylin shouted.

She began running faster now, spurred on by her friend's desperate cries. Noticing rooms she had never seen before, she yanked opened doors and stood in the doorways scanning the rooms. Looking for her friend, or some clue as to where she might be, or *something*.

Her eyes were suddenly drawn to a door at the end of the corridor. A blue wooden door with paint peeling in front of her eyes ad falling to the ground. The curls of paint making sharp, clipped sounds as they hit the floor, causing Kaylin to think of beetles scurrying across tile.

That's got to be it...

And she knew it was. Just like she knew it was late.

Just like she knew that none of this would end well.

In the real world, in the comfort of her bed, Kaylin clenched her fists. The look on her face the same as it was when she opened the door to her mum just a few hours before. Kaylin the Warrior. Ready.

Back in the dream she ran toward the door.

"I'm coming, Anni," she heard herself cry, registering the rage and fear in her own voice.

As she ran toward the door it stretched away from her into the distance. Then the floor tilted and she suddenly found herself running up a steep incline, her feet unable to grip the ground. She fell forward onto her hands, and realised why her shoes had no grips. The ground was slick with warm blood, oozing from beneath the door and sluicing down towards her.

Using reserves of energy she wasn't aware she possessed, she fought to keep going, keep going. Annika needs her, and she knows her friend isn't good with confrontation. Kaylin is the fighter, she'll protect her.

She half-ran, half-crawled for what felt like an eternity, eventually managing to somehow reach the door.

She lurched forward and grabbed the handle, her finger wet and slippery with blood but somehow managing to hold on.

In the split second it took her to turn the handle, she felt an almost uncontrollable urge to stop and go back.

Something in her mind knew this was a door she shouldn't open. The emotion wasn't strong enough to stop her opening the door, but the thought was strong enough to register.

Strong enough so that when she did open the door, she felt she should have listened to that voice.

Violently jerking the door open, she sees a small room with painted brick walls and a cement floor. There was no blood on her hands, or her feet, or anywhere else now, but she felt a sharp stab at the side of her head.

A trickle of warm fluid ran down from her temple, tickling her cheek on the way. She didn't need to touch it to know it was blood. And she didn't need to hear a gunshot to know what caused the sharp pain in her head.

Kaylin looked into the centre of the room and felt as though she'd been punched in the stomach. In the centre of the room sat not Annika, but Kaylin's mum. Tied to a chair and trying to scream – which was a pointless exercise due to the tape across her mouth.

Back in her bedroom, Kaylin's entire body tensed and her back arched almost impossibly high. A heart attack victim being defibrillated.

In the dream Kaylin ran over to her mum, powerless to stop the murderous feelings raging through her soul. She would kill whoever did this.

She reached her mum and registered that same look in her mum's eyes that she had seen a few hours ago in her mum's bedroom.

Except it wasn't just confusion this time, it was also fear. Her mum was scared. Scared of her.

As Kaylin pulled off the tape she heard a ringing noise and felt a force pulling her backwards, as though she was tied with a bungee cord to some immovable object behind her.

She sprang backwards, the door slammed, and her mum began to scream.

Kaylin jerked awake, momentarily disorientated and with every heartbeat feeling like a new explosion inside her chest.

The dream was over. But if it was over...

Why can I still hear screaming?

She sat up, back in reality now and immediately recognising the source of the screaming.

Mum!

"Mum!" she shouted, and ran out of her room in a mirror of her dream.

She realised that the horrific noise was coming from the sofa, and rushed around to face whatever she needed to face.

"Mum!" she shouted again.

Her mum lay on the sofa, holding a telephone to her chest and screaming at the top of her lungs.

"I did it!" she shouted at her daughter. "I really did it!"

Another high-pitched scream.

It took only around three seconds for Kaylin to realise that her mum wasn't screaming from pain or fear, but from joy. They were three of the longest seconds of her life

"I did it Kay!" her mum repeated triumphantly.

Kaylin's heart thundered away as it had done back in her dream, and her breathing was uncomfortably fast and shallow. It was clear that her body hadn't understood that there was no emergency as quickly as her mind had. Although the huge bruise distorting her mum's face wasn't helping her to calm down.

"What? Mum... I was asleep and in the dream, you... what's ha-"

"I'll tell you! I just got a call from a casting director who says he's heard great things about me and wants to see me! I'm meeting him in the West End! This is it, Kay! Jacuzzi here we come!"

Kaylin shook her head sadly and tried to catch her breath. How many more times would she have to have these adrenalin surges for nothing? That tsunami of fear and protectiveness, wasted on nothing. Maybe it as her fault, maybe she shouldn't worry so much all the time. Her mum was an adult after all.

Although I'm the only one who acts like one...

Her mind flashed back to the night before and the total love she'd felt for her mum.

Anger, then fear, then protectiveness, then guilt. She should be used to the order of these emotions by now but...

Her mum gave a girlish squeal and beamed at her daughter.

"Mum! Stop it!"

"But this is it Kay! This is it!"

"But I thought... you were screaming, and..."

Kimberley's smile suddenly dropped.

"What is it? You thought what?"

"The news on television. That man. Those actresses..."

Her voice trailed off as images of her dream came back to assault her.

"Oh Kaylin!" Kimberley said, and jumped up from the sofa. "Come here."

Her arms folded around Kaylin in that love-envelope all over again.

"I'm sorry, Kay. I didn't think. I just... I'm sorry Kay."

"I thought something might be happening..."

"Oh I know, Kay. I can see why you'd be scared. Someone else told me about that man as well so I already knew. Thank you for warning me though Kaylin. And I should've thought. I just got caught up in everything."

"It's ok, mum," Kaylin said, feeling slightly sheepish. Maybe her mum was changing for the better after all.

"No, Kay. After last night it's not ok."

Kimberley let go of Kaylin and moved back slightly so as to look her directly in the eye.

"Kay, last night I decided something. I decided that no more people will be coming to this house for meetings. Alright? I'm not going to invite anyone else around here. And now that I've had this phone call it means things are really happening for me. For us! So I don't need any more extra work anyway. It's all working out Kay. It'll be amazing, I promise."

Kaylin felt better despite the fact that her mum still wasn't being totally honest with her. Nobody ever came round for ##meetings#. Although she supposed it didn't matter what euphemism her mum used, the important thing was that she wouldn't be doing any more of those horrible things with those men.

Or did she just mean she wouldn't do them here, but would continue somewhere else?

Kaylin didn't allow herself to pursue that thought, and instead focused on the positive.

Either way, there'll be no more men coming here. That's the main thing.

She smiled at her mum, even though she began to think she was deluding herself as much as her mum.

The thought suddenly occurred to her that her mum was both the source of, and the cure for, most of her life's problems.

Her mum pulled her into another hug, and Kaylin leaned into her and allowed any negativity to drift away. There was no feeling in the world like being hugged by her mum. Whether she felt older than her years or not, she was still only fourteen.

"I trust you, mum. And I know it'll be amazing."

She felt her mum squeeze her tighter, and they stayed like that until they both felt better. A mutual – but surely temporary? - healing.

Kimberley let go and began walking to her bedroom, all the while telling Kaylin about the phone call and what an incredible opportunity it all was.

"*They* phoned *me* Kay, that means they really want me. Forget that stupid French film, they can keep it! This is it Kay, this is really it!"

Kaylin still remained unconvinced, but didn't let her mum know. After all was said and done, they'd both fallen back into their familiar roles - Mum The Dreamer, Kaylin The Actress.

They spoke while Kaylin got dressed and got her bag ready for school. Her mum told her not to worry, that she was meeting this man in a very public place and was good at reading between the lines with people. The former put Kaylin's mind at rest, the latter didn't because she knew it simply wasn't true.

Kaylin left for school, her mum standing at the door and waving, the smile still very much fixed to her face.

As Kaylin began her journey her mind flashed back to her dream, vivid images assaulting her without warning.

She'd forgotten most of what had happened, but the emotions it had caused were still there. Fear.

Terror.

An image of the room was burned into her mind, and she could still hear the screams ricocheting around her that little cell. And had her head been bleeding? She seemed to remember being stabbed or shot in the head, or was she imagining that part?

The sights and sounds of the dream bounced around inside her head until she was a few minutes away from home, at which point the images began to fade.

The sounds stayed with her until she walked through the school gates. At which point they stopped echoing.

And started screaming.

Fifteen

If a poll of the most disgusting places to work in the country was ever carried out, David Haldane's office would have to rank up there with the best – or worst - of them.

It wasn't disgusting because it wasn't clean – it was *always* clean – but because it looked like it'd been decorated by someone with too much money and too little taste.

And it had. David.

The walls and deep luxurious carpet were perfectly matching shades of rich dark brown, making it unclear where the walls stopped and the floor began. If it wasn't for the gargantuan window overlooking the city of London a visitor would be forgiven for thinking they'd walked into a cave.

Against the far wall was an oversized leather sofa, the colour of which could only be described as *double cream that'll probably give you a stomach ache*, and adjacent to that was an armchair which was also cream but a slightly lighter shade for some inexplicable reason. If that wasn't nausea-inducing enough, the leather chair behind the desk was yet another shade of cream.

And what a desk it was – a gargantuan, dark wooden console in the centre of the room, with mint-green leather panels spaced out in irregular intervals. David had been told that green gave offices a dynamic feel, breaking up the boring monotony of most premises. This was also the reason David had green curtains hanging either side of the window.

Dark browns, three different types of cream, and mint.

David was clever, a creative genius some would say, but not once had it occurred to him that his office looked like an explosion at a chocolate factory.

Today, the usually pristine office looked slightly untidy, thanks to the stacks of newspapers piled up on the normally impeccably ordered desk.

David sat in his big cream chair at his boat-like desk and flicked through one of the newspapers. He'd been working his way through the pile all morning, searching for something, anything that would help him get an exclusive on this whole Artist thing.

For forty-eight hours he'd done little else but obsesses about this man. Who was he? Where did he come from? Why was he killing actresses? Why not actors too? Maybe he hated all women, or maybe he *loved* all women and this was his perverse way of showing it?

The first time David had heard about the murders he didn't think much of this Artist character. He was probably some run of the mill, average loser who'd never had a girlfriend and was angry about it. He was probably weak, hitting out at soft targets rather than going after someone who might actually be able to fight back. Drugging someone, tying them to a chair and shooting them from a distance wasn't fighting.

David's office was situated directly behind one of the newsroom studios, which was one of the areas no well and truly within the remit of his job role. He didn't love the location of the office – he always felt his staff would think he chose it so he could monitor them merely by stepping out of his office. But then the entire building and its layout was unconventional. It could've been worse, he supposed. They could've given him an office in the newsroom.

He had three teams dedicated to the Artist story, who worked on it exclusively. He had reporters, investigators, journalists. All of them clamouring for an angle that hadn't already been covered, either by a competitor or by the police.

He had to get *something*, make his mark in the industry. Earn his keep.

David wasn't a young man, although he certainly wasn't as old as others who had been promoted to his position either. The reason for his high status role was simple. David Haldane was good, *exceptionally* good. Although he was all too aware that he'd had a run of bad luck recently and was on very thin ice with the powers-that-be.

All the other major channels had broken the story about the current Miss. World and Oliver Murphy - the so called 'Beauty and the Beast' case - a full hour before him. And even before that, his main competitors at the NJN studios had broken the big one, the *really* big one, the *story du mois* as his first boss used to say. It was the outcome of the London Transport contract negotiations, the results of which would determine not only the future of London Transport, but very possibly the future of London and its entire infrastructure. David had been following the story for months, as had the rest of the country, but unfortunately for him his sources weren't as well placed as those of his rivals.

In short, he got the story second.

Now second wasn't bad by usual standards. Second is silver, which still beats the shit out of bronze and all the losers. But it wasn't gold. And if you're a newly-promoted member of a very exclusive and well-paid staff who everyone was looking at to deliver the story fast, gold was the only thing that mattered.

Another embarrassing moment for David Haldane. Another raft of whispers amongst his peers that maybe he just isn't that good anymore. That maybe he never was that good now you mention it, and I reckon he got promoted too young and came up too soon if I'm being honest I mean I like him and everything but if he's not producing results then there's only one place left for him to go...

His failures branded him. They marked him as a complacent man. And that wasn't like David at all, in fact he'd been promoted precisely because of his drive and spot-on gut instincts. He missed nothing, he was an eagle. But now...now he needed a story. A massive story. *The* story.

And if I don't find one soon...

He didn't dare finish the thought.

A day earlier, his boss had swanned into his office, screwing up his face at the decor - as he always did - and sitting in David's chair - as he always did. A power move, as if it were needed. Then he commenced his little monologue, the message coming through loud and clear. ##You're sinking, learn to swim again or get out of the pool.#

It was Thursday today. Every hour since the start of this Artist thing he'd been scouring the papers, speaking to his contacts in the police, even calling up forensic psychiatrists. And he'd got precisely nowhere. According to the source, there hadn't been enough murders yet to establish many facts about the killer or any kind of real pattern.

He seemed to work alone, but not necessarily.

He hated actresses but nobody knew why. Or did he hate all women, as David suspected? Was the whole Artist thing a lie, and this man just wanted fame for himself?

Was he making some point about the pursuit of fame, or was this all just an excuse for bloodshed?

Too many questions, not enough answers. Just another day for David Haldane.

Soon after the first tape had emerged, David very public offered £50,000 of *his own money* for anybody with information leading to the arrest or capture of the Artist.

This was the story of the moment and he wanted to make it his own. He wanted 'The Artist' to be forever linked with 'David Haldane' – the man who found the killer. The man who'd make Michael Assante forever grateful, and forever happy that he'd had the good sense to promote a man like David. And a grateful and happy rich tycoon as a boss could only bring good things for David.

But first, David had to take the steps necessary to actually find something out about this killer that nobody else knew.

Or maybe even uncover him. He felt a flutter in his chest at that.

Reenergised now, he threw the newspaper onto the floor and picked up another one. Rifling through and trying to spot what everyone else had missed.

His plan was the same every day – scan the papers in the morning, then the internet throughout the day. He needed to pick up the scent, and the only way to do that was to consume as much information as he could.

Not that there was every much variation from one news article to the other. Facts were facts, everything else was guesswork and conjecture. And as ever there was too much of one, and not enough of the other.

Wanting to maximise his time, David's attention turned to the television.

Television was, after all, an old friend. He'd made his name in television news, although as much as it'd given him he still felt it owed him more. He'd invested too much of his life into it to feel any other way.

Maybe the competitors could give him some clue, some inspiration, some lead to follow. Or at least give him the old drive back. He'd lost something along the way, he needed the hunger back. David Haldane existed to push himself and think of an angle that nobody else could. David Haldane existed to beat the competition.

In short, to *win*.

He pushed aside the scattered newspapers, found the remote control and switched on the plasma screens. He had four on the wall of the office, just above the nougat – or cream or whatever colour he decided it was today - sofa. He flicked channels like a bored child. Going from one channel to the other, pausing for only a few seconds at each station. None of it was new. It was heartening in a way – it meant nobody was a step ahead of him.

Although it obviously also meant he was on the same level as them, which is not what he wanted.

He angrily switched all four of the screens off and dropped the remote onto the discarded newspapers.

What was he *doing*? He needed an exclusive, not a rehashed piece of news from another channel or a newspaper. What was he, some teenage blogger hoping to impress his friends?!

These were the acts of a desperate man, not the confident decisions of a leader.

He put his head in his hands and rubbed his tired eyes. The cracks were beginning to show. Yes, he earned a stupid amount of money each year, but with that came more stress than he'd ever experienced in his life.

Just when he was beginning to wonder if he was still cut out for this at all, the phone rang.

He reached forward and picked up the receiver.

"David Haldane speaking."

"Dave. It's me. You won't believe what we've just found..."

As David listened to his old friend – his old Detective Constable friend – telling him about the discovery of yet another video, he smiled.

He grabbed a pen and scribbled down the address, then hung up the phone. He leapt up from his desk, grabbed his jacket, and ran out of the chocolate office.

The exclusive was just around the corner, he could feel it. He wallowed in the feeling, allowing what was to be certain victory to infuse him with the vigour he'd sorely needed.

I'm back.

David Haldane is back!

He jumped in his car and sped off.

***

Thirty miles away the Artist also sits in an office that could double as a cave.

Searching the internet for details about the crimes, trying to find out what they know, what they think is happening, if they're getting close. Who they think the Artist is.

In all the internet searches and various true-crime forums one name keeps cropping up. A name The Artist has never heard of before.

David Haldane.

He seemed to be forcing himself into every item, every article on *Andy the Artist*, making comments and giving one sound bite after another.

These are the pages Andy returns to again and again.

Very concerned... public awareness... £50,000 reward... my own pocket... we need to find and stop him... killing innocents...

The Artist smiles. Clearly the murders are working. People are taking notice and the actresses are getting their fifteen minutes. And then some.

The Artist reads on.

David Haldane spoke about 'Andy'... written by David Haldane... David Haldane gives his opinion...

It was interesting and not coincidental that this man's name was turning up so many times.

Too many times.

He obviously wants to be included, wants to be a part of this production.

Someone's trying to get a bit of their own fame by aligning themselves with me.

Trying to link us together? Do you want to be linked with me, Mr. Haldane?

Do you want your fifteen minutes too?

The Artist leans back, eyes staring at the picture of David on the computer monitor. It's a crude picture, not of as high a quality as the actresses' headshots, but it shows him clearly enough. The Artist reckons he is around forty, with curly black hair that is greying unevenly at the temples. Slightly overweight, but generally healthy it seems.

Another fat cat executive, yes? Making money from putting other people on television, yes?

Ok, Mr David Haldane. You've got my attention.

Welcome to the cast...

Sixteen

Kimberly stood on the train platform and waited. It had been a full three minutes since the man by the ticket machine had gasped at the bruise on her face, and she'd spent that time fighting to keep herself calm and focussed on her goal.

Yes, she felt self-conscious and yes, maybe she didn't look her best, but this was about her career. She had an audition to get to and she would get to it. No matter what.

Let them look, let them laugh. When I'm on the big screen they can look as much as they want, and I'll be laughing all the way to the bank. Kimberley Bellos does not give up.

As if on cue, the rumbling of the approaching train began. It started as a slight vibration, a distant hum which was felt before it was heard. Then the noise began, drums before a battle, the distant army getting closer and louder and stronger and meaner. Then a final, deafening roar, the battle cry.

As the train burst into the station, determination flooded Kimberley's body as if her heart was no longer pumping blood but molten steel. This was a battle alright, and she would be the victor. From now on, she would win.

The train slowed to a screeching stop, the doors whooshing open. She stepped inside and took a seat.

The train trundled then raced then roared onwards. Another battle-cry, another fight. And Kimberley was its centre.

She checked her watch.

It was exactly one-fifteen, which gave her around forty-five minutes.

She looked up at the tube map on the wall of the carriage and looked at the route she'd looked at a million times at home already. Wood Green to Piccadilly Circus. Twelve stops in total. She had enough time.

And she was ready. This time would be different.

It certainly *felt* different.

She exhaled loudly and fully, trying to control her breathing like one of her acting teachers had taught her. It nearly worked, although there was still a slight quiver in her breath, like a child who'd been crying at school whose breath sporadically catches in their throat at night.

Her mind drifted to Kaylin. A child crying. Or, in this case, a child sighing.

She wondered why her only daughter seemed to sigh all the time. Their life wasn't that bad. Surely she wasn't *that* bad of a mother?

She knew where thoughts like that would lead and so cut it off quickly. Being introspective had its place, and travelling to meet with a producer wasn't one of them. All her previous concerns about Kaylin always seemed to end up at the same source – herself. It made her angry about her life.

And angry at herself.

She tried thinking about other things – acting credits to mention today, her favourite films, advice from acting teachers about getting work - but her mind kept sliding back to Kaylin.

Her daughter's life had been tough, it would be strange if she *didn't* sigh a lot.

Why wouldn't she? No money – Kimberley's fault. No father – Kimberley's fault. Not allowed to sleep in her own bed all the time – Kimberley's fault. Not to mention the fact that she'd been exposed to all those men who came over. Those sleazy, horrible men with their illicit tastes, dirty fingernails, dirty little requests-

Her mental defences kicked in as she felt her thoughts becoming introspective again. She tried to flood her mind with inconsequential things, wondering what stop was next, wondering how it got its name, checking her watch again, touching her bruise to see if it'd gone down.

Her eyes scanned the map again. She wasn't even looking this time, just searching for something, *anything* to switch her train of thought. Her eyes flitted around the carriage. There wasn't exactly much to see.

The train slowed as it entered the next station, and she found something.

Plastered on the platform wall was a huge film poster. It was a re-release of one of her favourites, one of those little independent films that dies at the box office but becomes a cult classic amongst drama students. Just seeing the poster had an effect on her.

Had *that* effect on her.

That effect which overpowers, as it always did and as it always would to anyone with ambition. Total and complete submission to an unknown emotion, an addiction to *that* feeling.

She never understood what *that* was, she just knew it drove her. It was behind her ambition, which was behind everything else. It was the feeling that superseded every other. An emotion that didn't just turn down the volume on everything else, but engulfed and destroyed it.

Nothing was more powerful, not even the love of a mother for her daughter...

Like the emotions of a woman in love inhaling *his* aftershave, or a victim going back to *that* place, it was indescribable but unmistakable. Sometimes it was a sound that triggered it, sometimes a moment in a film, sometimes even walking past a theatre. Today, here and now, it was the poster.

She remembered a friend she'd known years ago, a stand-up comic who could never quite break through to real fame or success. He would speak about *that* feeling and how it slammed into him whenever he was about to go on stage, in those two or three moments just after his name was called out. He'd be walking up to the microphone, preparing for the battle about to ensue and he'd feel *it*, be strengthened by *it.*

Focussed by *that* feeling, *that* high.

His focus was comedy, Kimberley's was acting.

Or, to be more precise, fame.

She'd once tried to explain the feeling to an ex-boyfriend, a non-actor or 'civilian' as she half-jokingly referred to him. They were lying in bed just a few days after they'd met – patience was a virtue neither possessed – and she was telling him how it felt.

"It just feels like you just want to, I suppose you just want to express yourself. You want to like get up and just scream 'I'm here! Look at me! Look what I can do!' And... you want everyone to just pay attention and watch so you can...prove yourself and so that they'll see who you are. You just have like an itch, no, not an itch, like an #urge#. Like a real urge to just *dominate*. But not in a bad way, like hurting anyone. Proving yourself. Showing the world who you are. 'I'm here now. Stop everything and watch'. And nothing else matters, not anything that you've ever been through. It's like a total focus. It's like almost a rage, y'know, like you want to stand somewhere and just put your arms out and look up at the sky and scream and scream until they listen and notice and see who you are. And what you are, how great you are, and what...what all the others – #all# the others – have missed. It's like payback time. Like a scream coming straight out of you that they have to listen to. Like you can't be ignored anymore because you won't let them do it to you anymore. I don't know if this is making any sense..."

She remembered lifting her head from his chest to look at his face, to see if there was any spark of recognition there. He smiled at her and said he understood. But he didn't, she could see that. She slowly lowered her head and thought it didn't matter. She hadn't explained herself very well, and even if she had, would it change anything? She thought not.

How could she explain the unexplainable? And why would anybody really want to?

The train jolted and snapped her back into the present. She checked the map, nearly there.

The rest of her journey was spent daydreaming about the future. They were vivid, fantastical dreams, and she pushed reality out of her mind whenever it tried to interrupt.

The train stopped at Piccadilly Circus and the Dance of the London Tube began. People pushed and tutted at each other. Others avoided eye contact so as to avoid having to give up a seat for an old person who was getting on. Tourists with big bags, knocking everybody. Mothers with hyperactive children, making noise, eating sweets. More pushing, shoving and tutting. Others became indignant while exiting the tube, incredulous that anybody would dare get on before they themselves got off – but of course not daring to say anything. Just a withering look - behind the person's back - and a story to tell when they get home.

The London tube network. An underground city of ever-changing inhabitants with no ties, no loyalties, and nothing in common but location. Not unlike the city above that it serves.

Kimberley stepped onto the platform and tried her best to ignore the commotion swirling around her. She had a meeting to attend. The future was about to begin – society and its games could wait.

She rushed out of the tube station and walked to her destination, arriving five minutes early. The meeting place was a bar at the top of a bookshop overlooking central London. Not the most obvious place for a bar, but the view was incredible. A panoramic vista of London, encompassing the majesty of St Paul's Cathedral with the lights and bustle of Piccadilly Circus.

And – more importantly - the waiter who had seated her had called her 'Madam' too, so maybe some people in London did still have manners. Or maybe it was just the ones who worked for tips?

Once at the table she promptly ordered tonic water with a slice of lemon. Wine would have been good for her nerves, but not much else.

She waited.

And waited a bit more.

Her drink arrived, and she took a couple of sips.

Then waited again.

People came, people went. Students meeting to discuss essays, business types in suits working on their laptops, single people, couples, even an entire family at one point. Like a slower, more civilised version of the Dance of the London Tube.

Then more people came and went. Some looked happy, some looked sad, some looked as though they weren't sure either way.

As time relentlessly carried on, Kimberley felt her dream of her big break slowly fading. Like a fire starved of oxygen, still smouldering but gradually being extinguished.

After an hour and a half of being glared at by other customers and watched suspiciously by the staff, the fire was well and truly out.

The back of her neck steadily became hotter and hotter with embarrassment, but she'd still waited, deluding herself with one ridiculous excuse after another before finally conceding defeat.

Maybe he was in a meeting. Maybe he thought they said three o'clock, not two. Maybe he has to fly over from America and got delayed.

Or, maybe he came in, saw me, and turned around again...

She took some comfort in the fact that maybe it was the bruise on her face that put him off. It was possible that the film would be shooting soon and so they didn't want to wait for the bruise to subside. If that was the case, then maybe they'd keep her in mind for something else that came up in the future.

Another maybe, another delusion.

She liked the bruise explanation. It was something to hook the rejection onto. A shot of morphine to block the pain.

Deep down she knew it wasn't morphine at all. It was a placebo. But it still *worked* like morphine, it still stopped her hurting. She wasn't emotionally resilient enough to expose it all as a lie – not yet.

It was the bruise. Nothing else.

So why were tears pricking her eyes? Why was her lower lip trembling?

She took one last look around, paid the £15 bill (two tonic waters plus service charge – welcome to London, baby), and left with her head down. She may have been an actress, but that didn't mean she wanted *every* tear to be shared by the audience.

***

An hour later Kimberley was home, pacing around her bedroom. The entire journey back had consisted of replaying the arrangements for the meeting. She mentally checked the time, the location - even the day.

She toyed with the idea of phoning him, just to see if he had gone to the wrong place or been held up somewhere. Out of a sense of self-preservation she decided against it. She'd already been rejected once today, she didn't want to be further humiliated by having a bunch of lies chucked at her as well.

She curled up on her bed and closed her eyes. Her mind wandered and she began to play the 'what if?' game.

The game that nobody can ever win.

What if she hadn't gone today? What if she was a producer and the one making and breaking other people's careers? What if she had a real job?

What if she never cheated on her husband...?

She drifted off to sleep, thinking about life – both the way it was, about the way it could be.

Just at the point where sleep would totally disconnect her from the conscious world, her mind hovered around thoughts of her ex-husband. The face was hazy, which wasn't really any wonder. She hadn't seen him for the longest time, so he was bound to have changed.

Such a long time in fact that she doubted she'd even recognise him if he walked through the door.

***

Two miles away, Kimberley's potential employer gave up waiting. He paid the waitress, got up and stormed out of the café.

Seventeen

The Artist is angry. Resources have been wasted.

Scouring the internet, making phone calls, reading cover story after cover story, spending my time and money...

And now one of them doesn't turn up for me?! What kind of an actress doesn't turn up to a meeting with someone who is going to give them a chance?!

It's been an hour since the last one didn't bother to meet with the Artist, but time has done nothing to quell Andy's rage. Walking through Soho now - after waiting for nearly two hours - anger pulsing though veins.

I'm the answer to her problem! She wants fame, I was offering it to her on a silver platter! She would have been world famous.

No wonder none of them get anywhere. How can they get their big break if they can't even be bothered to meet with the people who want to give it to them? Idiots!

Now it's the Artist's turn to play the 'what if?' game.

What if I just choose someone else? What if I just go up to one of these people right here and ask them if they want to be famous, ask one of these idiots if they'd like fifteen minutes to show what they can do? To show this fucking planet how special they are, how fucking different and unique they are and how they're not like everyone else and how much more fucking important than everybody else they are? Give them the chance to be someone, which is what they all want! That's what they want!

Steps quickening as the anger mounts. Stomping the pavement. A monster charging through its prey.

She didn't turn up for me! *That bitch, that fame-whore!*

The Artist doesn't notice people moving out of the way, all of them sensing that today would not be a good day to block the path of this creature.

This is why I do what I do! This is why I am the Artist! They want fame, then they don't even bother to meet! Or have the common fucking courtesy to cancel.

A new plan hatches now, thoughts turning from defeat to victory.

Why wouldn't I take it out on another one of them? Why shouldn't *I? Why not punish one of them for something one of the others did? They're all the same after all.*

They all deserve what's coming to them...

The Artist reaches Tottenham Court Road, then turns and walks slowly towards Oxford Circus. No longer stomping now, but composed. And stalking.

The area is bustling with shoppers, buying gifts for their loved ones for Christmas. Couples hold hands and smile at private jokes, parents tell their kids to behave, "or Santa won't come this year!"

Santa never came for the Artist.

No, that wasn't true. He did come a few times, but then he stopped. All of a sudden *everything* stopped and nothing was good anymore. Santa became as silent as the body lying in the coffin.

As silent as *her* body lying in the coffin.

The Artist stops walking as the rage coursing through veins metamorphoses into sadness, flooding and overwhelming its host. The strength of anger becoming the desperation of anguish.

The Artist does not know, and never will know, how close this emotion is to *that* feeling. The urge, the *need*, to do something. To do anything to satisfy this desire, this compulsion, this *pain*. To stop it, to feed it, to do whatever it takes to rid the body of its terrible addiction. To make the pain go away.

The Artist is standing still as the friends, families and lovers walk past, oblivious to the dying, tortured soul in their midst.

Her body.

Her body lying in the coffin.

The Artist is screaming and shouting, tensing and twisting like a nest of cobras. But internally. All of the suffering is inside, where nobody could see. Inside where it always had been, where it always would be.

They couldn't see it, but they would feel it.

Everybody would feel it.

There was only one way to feed the need for vengeance now.

Find another one. Another one of these whores, ready to sell themselves to me. To fame.

Do it. Now.

The thoughts came thick and fast.

London. Drama schools scattered around. Television studios all over the place too. Theatres, of course. There must be auditions happening right now. Tens, maybe hundreds of them. Here, where the golden paving stones await.

Do it.

Do it now.

The Artist begins walking again, faster this time. The pace quickens, accelerated by a cruel excitement. The strong, controlled hand pulling a smartphone from a pocket, ready to search on the move.

Walking and peripherally watching, so it appears as if nothing is being seen. But everything is being seen.

Looking, scouring, hunting.

Where are you?

The Artist slides into the midst of people along Oxford Street. Just another shopper seeking that perfect gift.

Seeking that perfect actress.

I'll make you famous...

Eighteen

Kaylin dumped her schoolbag on the sofa.

"Mum! I'm home!"

Without waiting for a reply, she went into the kitchen intending to get some juice, and stopped short when she saw the whisky tumbler on the draining board. The glass hadn't been there this morning, and there was only one reason it'd be there now.

She took a deep breath, hoping she was mistaken, and that the glass had been there this morning. Or that her mum used it for a soft drink for a change.

She walked to her mum's bedroom and carefully knocked on the door.

"Mum?"

She heard a faint murmur from behind the door, as though she'd waken her mum.

Her stomach dropped. She knew her mum was either drunk or sleeping it off.

She slowly pushed the door open. Her mum was lying facedown on the bed, fully clothed.

"Mum?" she said. "Are you ok?"

Her mum mumbled something into the bed, and pushed herself up. She looked at her daughter and blinked a few times, like a creature coming out of a cave and into the light.

"Are you ok, mum?"

"What?" she asked, and then suddenly sat bolt upright. "I was asleep Kaylin. Do you have to come in and shout the house... shout the house down every time you get home?"

"Sorry mum."

"You always are," she slurred. "How about trying not to do anything to be sorry for next time?"

Kaylin didn't answer. Yet another rhetorical question, no need to reply. She saw the look on her mum's face, and her heart sank. A damaged ship plunging into the depths.

After their talk, after *that* hug, things had clearly reverted back to exactly how they always were.

Kaylin resigned herself to the truth. Her mum would never change.

"Sorry mum," she said flatly. "You're right. I'll try and behave next time."

She turned and went to her room, hoping her mum would calm down. Or sober up.

Fifteen minutes later, Kaylin heard a rustling noise outside her bedroom door. It was slightly ajar, so she stood and peeped through the gap between the door and the doorframe. Her mum was standing in the hallway, looking at herself in the mirror on the wall and very carefully touching her face.

Kaylin opened the door and began to ask her mum if she needed any ice for her bruise.

As soon as she'd started talking, Kimberley had jumped.

"For goodness sake, Kaylin! You scared the life out of me!"

"Sorry, mum," Kaylin said sheepishly. "I thought I could help."

Her mum abruptly stopped looking at herself in the mirror and turned defiantly to Kaylin.

"I'm more than capable of getting my own ice, Kaylin. Stop interfering."

"Sorry mum," she said for what felt like the hundredth time.

An awkward silence hung between them.

Kaylin knew the audition couldn't have gone well, but thought her mum might want to talk about it.

"How did everything go today, mum?"

"What do you mean?"

"The audition."

"The audition?! What audition, Kay? He didn't turn up, did he?"

"Oh, mum..."

Kaylin watched as her mum's facial expression went from exasperation to rage.

"Don't feel sorry for me, Kay! I'm fine, they're the ones that are losing out! One day they'll be begging to take me on and do you know what I'll say to all of them? Forget it! If you didn't want me then, then you can't have me now!"

Kaylin was mentally running through a list of responses, trying to find the most appropriate thing to say. Desperately scouring her mind for something to say that would tell her mum she was here, but not in a patronising way. Not in a way that would make her feel worse.

Then-

"Anyway that's all history now. I've got somebody coming over tonight about a different film, so you'll have to stay at Annika's."

Her voice was defiant, her body language even more so. It said, 'I'm the parent, I know what's best, and don't you dare think otherwise.'

The awkward silence still hung in between them, worse than it ever had been, taunting them both.

"Mum, I-"

"What, Kaylin? What?"

"I... can't stay at Anni's tonight."

"Why not?"

"She's going out. They all are. I think it's her gran's birthday, or her aunt's. But they're all going out mum."

"Well someone else then. It's only for one night Kay. You've done it before."

Kaylin mumbled a response.

"What?!" Kimberley snapped. "Speak up Kaylin, I can't hear you when you-"

"I said there isn't anybody else."

The weight of the deafening silence hung heavy around both their necks.

Kaylin noticed her mum avoiding eye contact now, and she seemed to be thinking deeply about what Kaylin had said.

Kaylin wondered if she was thinking about the other night, and the promises she'd made. Not only would she be going back on those, but did she really expect Kaylin to stay home and be in the next room?

Kimberley looked toward Kaylin, but Kaylin got the sense that she wasn't looking at her, but #through# her. Calculating something, or weighing up her options.

"Well then," she said in a tone somewhere between unsure and defiant, "you'll just have to stay in your room."

"But-"

"Stay in your room Kay. That's it."

Neither of them moved, and Kaylin noticed her mum's facial expression changing. She looked almost curious.

"Sometimes," she said quietly, "you look at me like your father used to. It's like you're sad, but also like you hate me. I'm doing what I can for us, Kaylin. And I'm the parent here. So you'll do what I say."

With that, she went back into her bedroom and shut the door.

Kaylin stood looking at the spot where her mother had just been standing, almost trying to decide whether what her mother had just said was real or not. Had she imagined it? Surely she had. Why had she spoken about Kaylin's dad?

And she'd always lied to her about what she did with those men, if she expected Kaylin to stay home then there'd be no pretence left. She couldn't honestly mean that she wanted her daughter to be in the next room this time, could she?

A few hours later, she got her answer.

Nineteen

About an hour before he arrived, Kimberley told Kaylin that a man named Jimmy would be coming over.

All pretence of an innocent explanation was shattered as her mum explained that he was 'a good client' and so she needed to stay out of their way and keep quiet.

She neglected to tell her daughter that Jimmy was the one responsible for the bruise, for obvious reasons.

Kaylin nodded as her mum dished out the instructions for the evening, running through a list of things to remember – be silent, don't use the phone, don't pick up the phone if it rings, and don't touch the bedroom door as there's no lock on it.

She noticed a change in her mother's demeanour now, less defiant than before and slightly uncertain. Kaylin herself was still dazed and more than terrified about what she was about to witness. If not visually, then most likely through the paper-thin walls of their bedrooms.

When the doorbell rang, the noise shot through Kaylin like electricity.

Her mum rushed out of her bedroom.

"Stay in your room Kay. And don't make a sound. Ok?"

Kaylin nodded again, although felt so detached from reality she wasn't sure what she was agreeing to anymore.

She went to her room, closed the door and lay on her bed.

"Hello," her mum said. The speech was mumbled, but Kaylin could still tell her mum was trying to be sultry.

"Hi Kim-Kim."

That must be Jimmy.

"Sorry about the other night baby. I just... you know..."

"I know, baby."

The other night? What happened the other-

The thought smashed into Kaylin like a sledgehammer through a window.

Mum's face. The other night.

Mum's face!

The sledgehammer swung again, crashing into the window frame this time and smashing off pieces of wood and plaster like shrapnel.

The rage was returning, the anger rising.

Kaylin stared at the door. Inside her a battle was beginning. A rabid beast was fighting against its restraints, struggling to escape.

A kind of panic took over her. Like having to view a mangled body in the morgue, terrified not only about seeing the corpse itself, but about the consequences of it. The nightmares, the flashbacks....

The battle within Kaylin continued, although she was able to keep the beast at bay. Deep down, she knew that her mum couldn't really be in ##danger#. Not really. That man killing actresses wouldn't risk doing it in someone's own flat. And not with a child in the place either.

Although he doesn't know I'm here.

She heard muffled voices, her mum telling Jimmy how good he looked, how much she liked the way he did that, how she deserved it the other night, how he should teach her a lesson for being so bad.

Kaylin tightly shut her eyes.

She didn't deserve it the other night!

Where's your self-respect mum?! Where are you in all this? This isn't you! This isn't my mum!

In those few moments Kaylin felt a unique kind of hatred for her mum. Her mind flashed back to what she had said earlier – that sometimes Kaylin looked at her the same way Kaylin's dad had done, with sadness and hate. Maybe he was onto something...

Not that she wanted anything bad to happen to her mum, although she allowed herself to concede that, if anything else did happen, it would be well and truly her fault.

A few minutes later, the noises began from the other room.

Heavy breathing. Grunting. Moaning.

Adrenalin surged, feeding the beast inside which threatened to explode out of Kaylin and into the world. It was inches away from breaking its bonds.

I can't leave, but I will not stay and listen to this.

She rolled over and lay face down on her bed - *I wonder if mum's in this position too...* - and wrapped the pillow around the back of her head. Trying to block out the sounds.

For a moment it seemed to work, and if Kaylin hummed slightly the vibrations blocked out the bulk of the noises. But she could still hear enough.

Bile rose in her throat, and she realised it wasn't his voice that was affecting her anymore, it was hers. That submissive tone, and the words she was using which made her sound worthless. She was acting as though she wanted to get hit, as though she deserved punishment.

And somewhere, Kaylin was beginning to think that she did. She'd invited this... #man#... into their home again after he'd already beaten her up. What did she expect?

But does that mean I'm on his side?

Noises getting louder, accompanied by rhythmic knocks.

Enough.

She stood up, staring at her closed door. The beast had broken its restraints and was pushing against the cage door now. It was nearly free, and was giving Kaylin a strange power. It was burning through her eyes like lasers and, unbeknownst to her - she had that look on her face again. That murderous look.

Her protective instincts were kicking in, but this time it wasn't her mum she was trying to protect, it was herself.

She fantasised about going into the kitchen, picking up a knife and going into her mum's bedroom...

But what then? Would I attack him?

Well, something had to be done. She couldn't take it for one more second.

I could just leave. Just open my door and leave.

The 'what if' game...

What if someone saw her? What if Jimmy took it out on her mum? What if he liked the idea of taking it out on *two* women instead of just one?

Kaylin smiled at that.

Some force inside her liked – *loved* – the idea of this man trying to hurt her. Because it wouldn't happen. Years of pent up rage and anger and frustration and hatred would be released onto him, and he wouldn't stand a chance. Kaylin began to feel a little sorry for this hypothetical version of him. He wouldn't know what hit him.

But what about mum? He might see me leaving and do something terrible to mum.

The beast inside her took on a voice now. Not an angry voice, but a logical, almost calming one. A sinister whisper, not a murderous rant.

(But she'd deserve it wouldn't she? She brought him here.)

Kaylin was taken aback by the voice in her head that was not her own. She recognised it as having to be some part of her own mind, albeit from somewhere deep that she'd never known about before. A place hidden from her mum, and from Annika, and - most of all - from herself.

She found herself arguing against the voice now.

She brought him here to get some money. She brought him here for me, to help me. To help us.

(Really? And did she have to keep you here so you could hear everything? Was that for you too?)

She didn't have a choice.

(We all have a choice)

No, we don't.

(We do. You know we do. Accept it. She likes being used. The rejections and the anguish and the problems and all the rest of it. She loves it, the drama queen. Why else would she do it?)

For me...

Kaylin heard laughing in her head. A mocking cackle from somewhere deep in her soul.

The groaning was getting louder, so was the creaking of the bed, and so was the laughter...

Block it out. Now.

Her eyes scanned the small room, desperately searching for some form of escape, or for some way of alleviating all of this. An idea, something, *any*thing. She scoured the small space, her eyes finding the clothes on her floor, the school bag, the desk.

All the while the noises were getting worse, in every way that they could.

As if the desperation fuelled her imagination, she found something.

Under her desk lay a radio that she hadn't used for almost two years. The last time she'd used it was when she'd come down with flu and listened to it at night. Having background noise helped her sleep for some reason.

Her mum had made her wear headphones so the noise wouldn't wake her up. She'd had a lot of auditions back then and wanted to get eight hours sleep every night so she'd look her very best. Kaylin knew her mum didn't want her daughter's runny nose to ruin her chances - this could be the break she'd been waiting for.

Some things never change.

Kaylin rushed over to the desk, reached underneath and pulled out the radio – all the while repeating a phrase in her head like a mantra – *please have batteries, please have batteries...*

She turned over the little radio and opened the battery compartment.

Yes...!

All she needed now were the headphones.

Block it out. Now.

She opened the desk drawers, rifling through the various papers and detritus that she'd hoarded. Rapidly scanning with her eyes and flicking junk around with her fingers, like a girl with a snake bite desperately searching for the antidote before it's too late.

Nothing.

Come on... come on... where are you?

A thought.

The wardrobe?

She rushed over, opened the wardrobe door and threw out the crumpled clothes heaped at the bottom. T-shirts and shorts from before her growth spurt, now strewn all over the bedroom floor.

An eternity later, she found the headphones.

She jumped back on her bed and fumbled with the radio, trying to plug in the headphones before the noises from the next room destroyed her. They'd already burrowed into her mind and taken root, she didn't want any more future scars from any more horrific memories.

She plugged in the headphones and twisted the dial, rapidly searching for a radio station. She remembered her mum telling her how much her dad had loved classical music, and so stopped when she got to one of the classical stations.

She'd been feeling strangely close to her dad recently, although wasn't sure why.

She turned the volume to maximum, so loud that in between the various instruments all outside noise was blocked out by an electronic hum.

She lay back on the bed and closed her eyes, imagining her dad was there with her. The thought comforted her, although she couldn't imagine why. She didn't question it though, comfort was what she wanted, she wasn't about to query the source.

The presenter introduced a piece of music and, as it began, she felt relief and a calm wash over her. The beast was slowly stepping back into its cage, ready to be safely locked away again.

A short while later, whether through the peaceful music or sheer exhaustion of constant adrenalin, she fell asleep.

What Kaylin Bellos didn't realise was that the very piece of music which comforted and soothed her was her dad's favourite.

By the time the orchestra had got a quarter of the way through Gershwin's Rhapsody in Blue, she was asleep. And even when the music reached its peaks, getting so loud it should've woken her up, it never did. Kaylin's mind was somewhere else now, and it'd only get back to reality when she could handle it.

And right now, reality was the last thing she needed.

Twenty

The basement.

The Artist sits alone.

The anger from earlier in the day is nearly sated, the addiction mostly quelled, though not completely.

Not yet. There's still more to do.

On the computer screen is the news, being broadcast over the internet.

The wonders of the internet...

The Artist smiles.

On the screen the pretty blonde reporter with the low-cut top and fake breasts is talking about the 'callous and cold blooded' killer who 'preys on young, innocent actresses'.

They do love their clichés...

Apparently the entire industry is extremely shaken up, whatever that means. So shaken in fact that three of the top British actors have recorded a plea to anyone with any information to come forward.

How nice of them to come down from Mount Olympus. How nice of them to speak to those mere mortals and ask for help.

The Artist swallows down the bile rising up. Cheeks flushing red with anger.

The arrogance of you fucking people!

As if anyone with information wouldn't come forward unless you appeared on television and asked them! With your fake sad eyes, and your practiced serious faces, and your lies. So many lies! You make me sick!

Don't you see, you're the lucky ones! You made it. Nobody else is going to. Stop lying to them all. It won't happen for them.

Stop ruining lives.

The reporter came back on armed with her most sombre facial expression. Well, the most sombre she could look after that amount of plastic surgery.

And you're even worse, at least actors know they're playing a role. At least they don't pretend they care.

The Artist leans closer to the screen, and speaks aloud.

"*Reporters?* You're actresses just like the rest of them! Why else would you be close to tears during reports on wars and famine, and then act as though you don't have a care in the world two seconds later when you're reporting on a dog that swam the channel, or some fucking parade about to come through London, or an old woman who's won nineteen baking competitions in a row or something equally fucking vacuous?!"

A number flashed up on the screen for any viewers to call with information.

The Artist smiles again.

As if anybody knows anything...

The reporter goes on, constantly referring to Andy the Artist simply as 'Andy'.

The Artist's smile drops. More shouting at the screen.

"No! Not 'Andy'! Andy the Artist! You don't know me well enough to call me Andy, my dear. You fucking idiots probably believe that Andy's my real name too, don't you? As if Mummy dearest and Daddy christened me with that name! As if I didn't give myself the title only after I'd earned it."

The Artist leans back from the screen and is silent again, trying to control the breathing that has become increasing shallow with anger.

You know nothing. But you will learn.

The Artist turns to the left and looks through the mirror.

She looks so peaceful.

Janet Leeson had been standing outside the Lipman Studios when Andy met her. She was pacing up and the down the road, smoking a cigarette, drinking water from a bottle and mouthing words from a sheet of white paper– universal sign language for 'actress waiting to go into an audition'.

Andy turned up – playing the producer role this time – and made friends. Which was surprisingly easy considering the entire industry is 'extremely shaken up'.

With this memory, a cruel smile now creeps onto the face of the Artist.

Janet went into the audition, and Andy walked to the tube station that she'd mentioned she'd be passing by after she was due to finish. Funny how a few carefully worded, casual questions can garner such useful information.

Half an hour later they met at the station - "How strange! That's so weird! How did it go?" - and Andy asked if she wanted to go out for a coffee somewhere locally. After all, "I'm sure we've both got a million audition horror stories, just from different sides of the fence!"

That was three hours ago. And this would be the horror story that Janet Leeson never gets to tell.

The yellow and purple alarm clock rings, breaking Andy's focus. The Artist places a hand on the plastic fried egg on the top of the clock and gently pushes down. The alarm stops immediately.

It's time.

The Artist leans over, switches on the camera and pushes the Record button. Then the Artist – truly an Artist - flicks another switch on the desk. An alarm rings in the next room, much louder than the first.

Janet jerks awake, and goes through the motions that all the others went through. Twitching, tensing, trying. Choking, hoping, crying.

Then, the intercom. Not only amplifying but also distorting the voice, so it is nothing like the voice that boomed at the television news only moments ago.

"The timer starts now. You have fifteen minutes. Make it count."

This was the best part. When they realise that their entire life comes down to only fifteen minutes. Not an Oscar acceptance speech, not a high profile wedding to another actor, not a lifetime achievement award.

Fifteen minutes.

Fifteen minutes of wondering if it was all worth it.

Was it worth living for this Janet?

Is it worth dying for?

Look at you now. Struggling like the others. Trying to protect your life. What life? The life you give so freely to others? The life you allow them to use, to manipulate, to change, to dominate, to destroy?

The life I will soon take from you.

And why not?

You so freely give others the chance to make or break you, well I'm doing both. You will be famous after this. I'm ensuring it.

Unfortunately you'll have to pay quite a price for that fame – your life.

But then, it's not really yours anymore is it?

Even if I wasn't controlling your situation now, somebody else would be. An agent, a director. Someone telling you to look more to the left, or lean more to the right, or cry more tears in that scene, or laugh harder at that joke.

I'm giving you everything you want and everything you fear. You cannot have one without the other.

And you no longer have a choice in the matter.

The Artist is standing now, staring at Janet Leeson though the mirror. Staring through cold eyes at the young actress.

Staring through a mask of twisted rage.

You have felt all your life that fame is your destiny. Well it is, Janet Leeson. You were right. And today you will meet that destiny.

The Artist coldly watches the terror of the young actress as the minutes tick by. No compassion creeps in, no pity. Nothing left but anger and hatred.

I am not doing this to you. You are doing this to you.

Even now somewhere in that one-track mind of yours you're thinking about how one day you'll use this in a scene, or how you'll make a script out of it. Or how you'll try to charm me if you get the opportunity.

Charm me and whore yourself to me to make me stop.

Whore yourself to me...

The alarm rings, breaking Andy's – the Artist's – thoughts.

It really is time now.

The Artist walks to the door, picking up the gun on the way out. The curtain is about to come down on this particular Act.

And, Janet, we wouldn't want to keep the audience waiting now would we?

Twenty One

Kaylin was jolted awake by the sound of a door slamming.

As was becoming the norm in her life, the negative emotions began weighing her down before her conscious mind had even begun to work. She felt physically and emotionally drained, and all before she even knew why.

She had no idea what time it was, but she was still wearing the headphones, although the batteries in the radio seemed to have died. Gershwin seemed like a long time ago.

Then the rest of the memories came flooding back.

Mum. That man. The noises.

Those noises...

She looked up at the ceiling. The ceiling she'd looked at night after sleepless night, hoping for something to happen to change her life for the best. Something big needed to happen. Things had been too bad for too long, something had to be done.

But what? What can I do?

The voice from last night answered, causing her to jump.

(You can't do anything.)

The tone was taunting, mocking.

Yes I can. There must be something.

(No. Nothing. It's not you who has to do something, it's her.)

Who?

(You know who...)

Mum?

(Yes. You can't do anything.)

No, that's not true. I can help. I can fight.

(Fight who?! And with what?! You're a little girl.)

I'm not. There must be something I can do. She's ruining both our lives.

Shame and guilt stabbed Kaylin's heart at that thought. It was what she believed, what she'd always believed. But she'd never admitted it before.

She sat up and took off the headphones, her ears feeling suddenly cold. She got off the bed – quietly, just in case #he# was still here – and put the radio back underneath the desk. All the while trying desperately to silence that terrible voice in her head.

I was wrong. It's not her fault.

(It is...)

No. It's not. They use her. All of them use her, it's not her fault.

(She lets them...)

She hasn't got a choice.

(She has. Everyone has -)

"No!"

For the second time Kaylin jumped, startled at her own voice and the power behind it. She froze, listening for any noises outside the room that suggested she'd been heard.

She didn't dare to move, holding her breath and straining to listen for any sounds.

Only one sound was audible, muffled and faint but unmistakable.

Her mum.

Crying.

(There is something you can do. There is. And you know what it is. Go in there and stop him. Stop him from hurting her. Protect her.)

All at once the energy returned to Kaylin, jolting through her body like multiple lightning strikes. Her muscles once more became the hardest steel, and the raging inferno once again burned through her eyes, into and beyond the closed door.

(Save her. Make him pay. He might be the one killing the actresses. Don't let it happen. Kill him. Do it. Do it now.)

Kaylin pulled the door open with more force than she knew she possessed. It slammed hard against her wardrobe, shaking it and causing the door to creak open.

She stepped out of her room, spun round and slammed herself into her mother's door, almost splintering the doorframe with the force.

The door banged open and Kaylin viewed the scene through murderous eyes.

Her mother was lying face down on the bed, crying into the pillow.

Where are you?

There was nobody else in the room.

Where is he?

Somewhere in the dark recesses of Kaylin's being, a memory emerged from the depths.

The door slamming.

He must have left.

Kaylin stood in the doorway, watching her mother cry, and tried to decide which emotion she should be feeling – she honestly didn't know anymore.

As time had gone on, and as her mother's crying had become more frequent, it affected Kaylin less. She was becoming accustomed to distressed people, and she didn't like the feeling one bit. She still felt deep sorrow, but slightly less than the time before, which was slightly less than the time before that.

Something was growing, readying itself to take the place of the sorrow. But what was it? It was too slight to pinpoint, but – anger? Was it anger?

(If she doesn't like being used, she should find something else to do. Get a real job and be a real mum.)

Kaylin shook her head sharply, and only once. The nervous twitch of a Tourette's patient. She was trying to silence the voice. Trying to remove reality from her situation. She didn't want to know her mum was crying, she didn't want to see it, and she certainly didn't want to feel angry about it anymore.

But she did. On all three counts she did.

Her mum moved slightly. She turned her body so that she was no longer face down but facing completely away from Kaylin. The bruise on her face was sore from the salty tears and facial contortions of her crying. She pulled the bedsheets up slightly.

If Kaylin could see her mum's face she would have seen a young child wrapped in a blanket, scared of the monsters underneath the bed.

Kaylin knew her mum didn't want her to see the tears, and that she was trying to protect her from yet another horrible sight.

Kaylin realised her anger had subsided without her noticing, and it was once again replaced by sorrow. The constantly changing emotions was draining to the young girl, fourteen years old and living in a bipolar world. Blown about by the wind, having to go wherever it cared to take her.

She went to the bed and lay on it behind her mum. Her arm slowly crawled around her mum's waist– almost as if she was afraid of breaking her delicate parent – and was met by Kimberley's hand grabbing on tight. Kaylin felt the soft pillow beneath her head and remembered the million times she'd lay here before. Happy times, sad times.

Mostly sad times.

She tried to stay focused on the hugs and the kisses, and all the other happy times though. Here. In this bed. With her mum.

(But who else has lain here?)

The voice came out of nowhere. Kaylin was well aware that it was her own internal voice, not some ghost or monster, but she was as powerless to stop it as if it were some creature outside of herself. She was definitely the one saying these things inside her mind, and she knew she was, but she still had no recollection of formulating the thoughts before they were voiced.

(Well? Who else?)

She closed her eyes. A surprisingly childish thing to do, but then what else was there to do?

(He lay here. *Not even an hour ago. And now you're lying in his place. The place of that... man.)*

Stop it.

(Get angry.)

No.

(Think about what they do with her. To her.)

Please...

(Please what? Please stop the truth? Look at her. Broken, bruised, almost totally ruined. If she was a horse they'd put her down. It'd be more humane. Is that killer really so bad? At least he's sparing all those others all of this.)

Tears pricked Kaylin's eyes. She felt them flowing from beneath her closed eyelids. How could she think such a thing? Yes, the thoughts felt like they were someone else's, but she knew they weren't. She knew that somewhere in her mind *she* had thought *that*. And about her own mum.

And as for sparing all those others... Yes, her mum's life wasn't perfect – it wasn't even close - but a terrible life is still a life.

Things can change. People change.

(But they won't. They go round and round and end up in the same place. There are two destinations – fame is one.)

As if on cue Kimberley sighed a loud, long sigh. As though her soul was on the precipice of giving up completely.

(What you are witnessing is the other. Which do you think is more likely to happen again and again?)

Kaylin sobbed. Her mother was sobbing too, she'd apparently lost the will and the energy to cry loudly anymore.

(They'd put her down, Kaylin...)

Kaylin's exhausted body began to melt into the mattress, sobbing at the same pace as her mum. After a short while they breathed almost simultaneously. The spaces between each breath slowing as they both drifted further from consciousness.

Kaylin's mind drifted all over. From the dream of the other night, to the Gershwin piece she'd fallen asleep to earlier. She even allowed herself to miss her dad, and wish he would come back and save them from all this.

Sleep finally took her into its depths, and as she drifted off she listened to her mum's breathing, smelled the aroma of her mum's hair, and came back to a particular phrase over and over and over.

They'd put her down, Kaylin...

They'd put her down...

Twenty Two

This part was always the most unpleasant.

The disposal.

The performer had served her purpose – putting on a death scene to be watched by millions. She will be famous. She has gone from performer to piece of art.

Now she has to be removed.

The Artist has already removed the restraints, now all that needs to be done is for the body to be moved and destroyed.

There is the faintest brown line on the floor where the last body was dragged from her seat. Like a gruesome version of the guidance lines that Adrian – the very first member of Andy's audience – followed along the floor of the post room (and still would follow, if only he felt well enough to return to work).

Andy hoisted the piece of art up from underneath the arms. Behind the piece, not in front. With great effort the body was manoeuvred and dragged out of the cell door.

The Artist never filmed this part. There was no need. People want the magic not the reality. Who wants to see behind the scenes? Why spoil the performance?

The Artist took the body to the usual place, disposed of it in the usual way, and then returned to the office. This process was always the most clinical, and always the part done with the maximum of haste and discomfort. There was no enjoyment to be had here. The instruments needed were all kept in a bag outside the office, The Artist didn't want to be reminded of such things and only dealt with them when it was absolutely necessary.

These things had to be done, however uncomfortable they made Andy.

Andy was after all an Artist, not a monster. And a true Artist would take no pleasure in destroying a piece of art, even after the exhibition.

The Artist finished and cleaned. The cleaning rituals bordered on obsessive compulsive. The gloves were removed and burned, the saws and scalpels washed three times each, the linen destroyed with the gloves, the Artist's clothes washed three times, even the bullet had to be located and destroyed. All vestiges of the piece were buried with it – with what was left of it.

There had to be no trace remaining. Except, of course, for the film itself.

The Artist always sat and watched the film after the cleaning and other necessary duties were finished. There was no sexual satisfaction in it, and no joy in seeing another human being suffer and die. The satisfaction came from knowing that justice was being done. That the injustices were somehow being balanced.

Usually at this point the Artist would scour the internet again, searching for another victim. But not this time. This time the next actress had already been located.

The Artist knew her, and knew her well.

The Artist did not smile. The final Act was getting too close, the end too near.

On the 21st of December, this would all be over.

It may have taken ten years to get to this point, but justice would be served.

Twenty Three

"Kaylin, come on."

Kaylin was slipping and sliding between reality and her dream, not completely sure what was real and what was merely a construct of her mind.

"You have to get up..."

The voice echoed around her head, distorted by her mind in its dream state. It sounded like it was coming from just outside the cell in which she was sitting. She groggily looked down and noticed her hands strapped to the chair. She looked up in a panic and a terrified girl in a wooden chair was looking back at her through a huge pane of glass. The girl was bound, and had thick black tape across her mouth.

Kaylin tried to scream and realised her own mouth was taped up. She jerked her head back and forth, trying to dislodge it, and noticed the girl across from her doing the same. She realised with a deep terror that she wasn't looking through glass, she was looking into a mirror.

The voice again, impossibly coming from both nowhere and everywhere.

"You're going to be late..."

She focussed, trying to recognise the voice. It was distant, she couldn't even be sure what is had said. Adrenalin surged through her veins as she fought against the restraints.

Someone appeared to her left, punching her left shoulder. No, not punching, pushing. As if trying to shove her off the chair.

"You're going to be late for school again!"

Is that mum? Where is she? Maybe she'll help me escape although only if she's not too busy she gets really busy sometimes because of her job and all the auditions she goes to she's an actre-

"*Kay!*"

The cell, the chair, the restraints disappeared. Kaylin opened her eyes and saw her mum standing next to the bed, pushing her shoulder apparently as an attempt to wake her.

"You're always late Kay! Those teachers already keep going on about your timekeeping, or lack of it should I say?"

In spite of the chastising words, her mother's face and tone were much kinder this morning, spoilt only by the ever-present bruise with its purple-green edges. Kaylin had always seen her mum as a very pretty woman – she'd always had a lot of male attention – which had served to make the injury seem even more of a violation.

"Ok mum," Kaylin said, rubbing at her eyes. She struggled to get up, and momentarily forgot why she'd been sleeping in her mother's bed.

"Mum?" she said quietly.

"Yes Kay?"

"Are you... I mean, do you feel ok?"

Her mother tried to keep a neutral expression of her face, but Kaylin could see a twinge of sadness at the question. There was a slight twitch in her brow, and an almost imperceptible twitch in her lips which told Kaylin that her question had struck her mother deeply.

"I'm fine," Kimberley said, trying to smile. She came and sat next to her daughter on the bed.

"And Kay," she said solemnly, "I'm sorry. Not just for last night but for all the other nights when you've had to stay with Anni as well. It won't happen again. I mean it this time, Kay. I promise."

Kaylin was a better actress than her mother, but even she couldn't hide the doubt she felt. It pulsed over her face for just a moment too long before Kaylin managed to check her emotions and put her mask back on.

Kimberley leaned closer to Kaylin.

"Kay, I know that I promised before. But I mean it, I do. I know I've been terrible and... everything. Well, not terrible, but... I could've been better that's all, and I know I could've. And I will be better. I will, Kay. I'm doing this for us. One day Kay, we'll be living right up there with the best of them. We'll be rich! And everything'll be ok."

She took Kaylin's hand.

"It'll be tough for a bit longer Kay, but I swear to you that last night will never happen again. Not in this house, or anywhere else for that matter. Ok?"

Kaylin nodded in spite of herself. She didn't believe her mum for a second, although she had no doubt that her mum truly believed what she was saying. Her mum was an actress who needed to act, she needed drama. She was also a mother who needed to feed her child and if she couldn't do that through acting, then...

Kimberley leaned in and hugged Kaylin.

In the years to come Kaylin would remember that embrace, it'd come to her every so often seemingly out of nowhere. Not just because she and her mum were to be parted so soon after, but because it felt so hollow to Kaylin. The hug was false for her, a parody of the real thing. It was irredeemably tainted by the knowledge that her mother would be breaking her promise and back doing what she always did in no time. Maybe even that very evening, for all Kaylin knew.

Something had been broken last night. It would take more than mere words and assurances to fix.

Kimberley let go of her daughter, and Kaylin noticed how relieved she looked.

She leaned over and kissed Kaylin's forehead, then walked to the bathroom. A few minutes later Kaylin heard the spray of the shower hitting the bath.

She sat in the silent room, listening to her mother moving in the other. In spite of everything it was a genuinely comforting sound, like switching on the radio in an empty house.

The phone rang, breaking the silence and snapping Kay back to reality.

Kaylin sighed, then stood up and lifted the handset.

"Hello?"

"Hello, Kimberley?" the voice was deep and male. It reminded Kaylin of the man who narrated the trailers in the cinema.

"She's a bit busy at the moment," Kaylin said, wondering if this would be the next 'client' mum would be seeing this evening.

"Well, I don't really have very much time I'm afraid. I'm a producer and I'd really appreciate speaking with her. I'll only be two minutes."

Then the voice uttered the phrase that would later stay with Kaylin for the rest of her life.

"I'll make it count."

Kaylin screwed up her face in amusement.

He's going to make what *count?!*

Weirdo...!

Kaylin's amusement was slightly tinged with concern, although she couldn't quite identify the reason.

Her mother rushed into the room, wet and wearing only a towel. She quickly took the phone from her daughter.

"Hello? This is Kim... Who is this?... Oh! Hi! Yes, I got your message!... Yes... Really?!"

She looked at Kaylin with the face of a child on Christmas morning.

Kaylin's heart was racing, although she had no idea why. Maybe the news reports about the murders were playing on her mind, or maybe just the fact that she knew at any given time her mother would be back to her old tricks – literally. There was a definite sense of alarm creeping into her mind, and the all too familiar feeling of rage was returning.

(Because it might be him.)

Who?

(You know who.)

It could be anyone.

(True. But it could be him. Kill him.)

What?!

Kaylin felt a shudder go through her body as thought of killing that man gave her a jolt of excitement. She resisted both the thought and the associated feeling, and felt a sick shock at the amount of pleasure she knew she'd get from it.

(Kill him.)

Who?!

(Him. On the phone. He might be the killer, so kill him first. Or, if he's not, he's still one of them. One of those agents, or producers, or whoever. It doesn't matter what the title is, does it? The only way to stop her going back to her old habits is to stop them.)

I don't – how does that make any sense?

(The only way she will stop getting hurt is if these people stop promising her things and then not delivering. They won't stop themselves. So you have to stop them. All of them.)

How can I stop all of them? This is stupid.

(No it isn't. But, yes, you can't stop all of them. This is true. Unless...)

What?

(Unless...)

Unless what?

(Well, either you stop all of them...)

Or?

(Or you stop her.*)*

Kaylin's head jerked violently, once, as she tried to force the thoughts out of her head. The thought had struck an emotional blow and left her reeling.

She managed to somehow shake then thoughts from her mind, although the emotional residue was still there.

There was no pleasure in these thoughts, just fear.

Fear at the prospect of something happening to her mum – by her own hand no less – and the fear that came with the knowledge that she had been thinking these things. No malevolent force, no supernatural powers, *her*. Kaylin Bellos.

She tried to compose herself and get back to normal. Her mum was still talking on the phone but could be off at any second.

"Tomorrow?... That's fine, I can do that... No, no, thank *you*... See you then."

Normally at this point Kimberley would jump up and down, and Kaylin would humour her. The whole play would start up again as it always had, and most likely always would.

But, to Kaylin's surprise, that's not what happened.

Kimberley was obviously excited – Kaylin could tell by the flush in her cheeks and the huge grin on her face - but she seemed to be restraining herself too.

Kaylin noticed this change and allowed herself to feel a slight sense of relief, although this was tinged with a sense of horror at what she had just been thinking about her mum. As her mother told her calmly and quietly about the audition, Kaylin smiled slightly.

She found herself listening to what her mum was saying and, incredibly, began believing for the first time in what felt like decades that things might actually be changing. And who knows, maybe this ##could# be her mum's big break?

The rage and fear she had felt disappeared into nothing more than a distant memory. Her mum seemed to be different now, more stable, more like a parent.

Kimberley finished telling Kaylin about the phone call and the potential role, and calmly walked back into the bathroom. Kaylin heard the shower start up again.

Kaylin stood up and went into her bedroom to get ready for school. As she left her mum's bedroom she looked at the calendar on her mum's wall. It was one of those cheap calendars with a different beach scene for each month of the year.

It was December 20th. Five days until Christmas. She wondered what Santa Claus had in store this year.

She heard her mum call out from the bathroom.

"What mum?"

Her mum repeated whatever she'd said, but her voice was lost in the sound of the shower.

"I can't hear you, mum!"

The shower was turned off.

"I said can you write down that producer's name so I don't forget?"

"Ok."

Kaylin went back into her mum's room and rummaged around for a pen. She couldn't find one that worked so picked up an old eyeliner from out of the bin. There was an old envelope – probably from an unpaid bill –

in there too, so she took it out as well. She walked over to the bathroom door so she could clearly hear what her mum was about to say.

"Kay? Are you ready?"

"Yes." Kaylin was leaning against the door, holding the eyeliner and paper as though about to take some kind of rubbing.

"His first name is Joe. And his second name is Cameron. Did you get that? Mr Joe Cameron?"

Kaylin wrote down the name, not knowing how much a part of her life it would soon become.

Twenty Four

The Artist is unhappy.

After connecting the wires, reading manuals and phoning premium rate numbers for professional advice, not much is happening. Except for an unresponsive monitor and an increasing desire to launch a fist through it.

The anger feels like it might take over again.

Sometimes the anger helped, most of the time it didn't. For strategies, for detailed plans like this one, nothing short of total, unimpeded focus would suffice. The mind needed to be clear, untainted by emotion.

What is the point in doing any of this if the final act won't ever get fucking finished?!

The Artist's muscular hands clench into tight fists, the knuckles turning white, the fingers pressing hard into the palms.

Looking at the various dials, the frequency seemed right, but the picture still looked slightly grainy. Faint snowy lines kept appearing and disappearing, disrupting the quality. This was no good. They had to see a completely clear picture, live from the cell. It wasn't going to be for very long, but it had to be perfect.

The Artist checks the output lead, maybe it's just dusty? Nothing. Andy replaces the output lead and switches the monitor back on. The picture isn't unclear anymore.

Now it's gone completely.

What?!

I've done everything RIGHT!

A fist bangs against the monitor, vibrating through it and into the floor. Veins throb in that muscular neck.

The Artist is getting even angrier. This isn't good, and that familiar feeling of the rage taking over is staring to creep in. Andy has become accustomed to this, and knows how to control it, although not completely. Something has to be done right now, at this point, while thoughts are still coming clearly.

The Artist switches off the monitor and camera, leaves the leads and electronic equipment where they are, stands up and switches on the CD player.

Track Fourteen. Rhapsody In Blue by George Gershwin.

Time to relax.

Andy switches on the television, and also the video player now.

The video contains the first three Acts, which Andy now settles down to watch, quickly taking a seat as though not wanting to miss the beginning.

Justice, justice, and justice.

I've showed them three times, and will continue to do so.

And tomorrow, the last Act.

I will show them everything.

The thought keeps returning that maybe more should die, maybe more of them should be taught a lesson. But that thinking never leads to anything. For a start, how many could be killed, realistically? Even if it was ten or twelve, that's still only ten or twelve out of a million. The numbers aren't what's important, it's the idea behind it all, the message.

The lesson.

Not to kill all *of them, but to make examples of some of them so the rest will understand.*

Three lives for three lives.

And then a final one – a bonus life – to complete the production. A grand finale to drive the point home to these people. This 'industry'...

To show I am a true Artist.

The Artist.

Let's see how Mr David Haldane likes this particular little connection with me...

The Artist is calmer now. The combination of the music and video helping to reduce the tension.

The Artist glances over at the cables, wires and other electronic equipment lying on the floor, although still watching the video peripherally.

This has to work.

Even if it takes all night, even if I don't finish until seconds before the curtains comes up on the last Act.

Tomorrow is the culmination of everything. This has to be done. Or what has my life been for?

They will be avenged.

We *will be avenged.*

The video is playing in the background. The sound is muted, and the images of three young, beautiful girls gagged and restrained, wrenching and flexing, twisting and tensing, desperately fighting for their lives, is even more horrific viewed alongside the genius and timeless beauty of Gershwin's Rhapsody.

The Artist walks back over to the wires - still watching the first three Acts peripherally, still leaving some focus on the screen.

On the Art.

The music is helping a lot. It always sounded like the end of the world. Building to its crescendo, building up and building up. As though it were so beautiful, so elegant, that nothing that came after it could possibly live up to it. As though everything that followed would be a distant second to this powerful first.

Music to die for. And to kill for.

The Artist glances at the alarm clock – a ridiculously out of place yellow joke with a purple face. It is still early.

I've got time.

Time.

The Artist allows a smile. Then, a few moments later, laughter.

Time! I've got all the time in the world now!

Now, full-throated laughter. A sickening sound juxtaposed with the desperate scenes being played out on the screen.

I've got all the time that I need!

The maniacal laughter fills into the room, seeping into every corner, bleeding into the darkest parts of it and dissolving the sound of the Gershwin piece like acid through flesh.

I've got time. All I have to do is make it count.

And in twenty-four hours, that's just what Andy the Artist intends to do.

Twenty Five

Things are different this time.

It was the third that the thought had occurred to Kimberley, the third time she'd felt a strange sort of calm wash over her. Things felt different because she felt more realistic now, more in control.

She was sitting on the sofa, alone. Kaylin was at school, and Kimberley was taking the opportunity to evaluate her life. She needed to make a plan about how things would be from now on.

No more selling herself. No more mood swings. No more instability for poor Kaylin.

She would be a good actress and a good mother from now on, that's the way it needs to be.

In the deep, dark recesses of her subconscious mind there was an acknowledgement that she'd decided to be an actress *first*, and a mother *second.* But it was too slight a thought, buried too deep to bubble up into consciousness.

Kimberley fought the urge to get too excited about her resolutions. She allowed herself to feel a slight enthusiasm but that was all. It was actions that counted now; she had to prove to Kaylin – and to herself – that she was going to do things differently from now on.

She thought about the audition of the next day. It felt very much like the calm before the storm.

Well, not the storm, but what if tomorrow is it? What if tomorrow really is the one? This could be it this time.

She saw an image of herself teetering on the brink of eternity, standing at the edge of the universe. If she looked down she could see the planets, the stars, the galaxies, everything. And it was all for her. All she had to do was reach down and scoop them up.

Everything she ever wanted could really be that close.

And she knew she shouldn't get too excited but it just felt so *close* this time.

She didn't remember ever feeling like this before, although in truth she knew that she must have done.

Every so often, with a handful of auditions, she would feel that something apocalyptic was about to happen. As if the universe was willing her to go to and meet a certain casting director because it was her turn in the spotlight.

All those other times, she'd only start feeling this way an hour or so before the audition itself though. There had started to be a *why not give it a try* element to most auditions she'd been to recently, as though she supposed that she may as well go on the off chance it might lead somewhere.

But this one definitely felt different.

And what if that feeling was right? What if the audition tomorrow would be the one that she'd be talking to a chat show host about this time next year? Sitting next to Alisters and talking about how what an honour it was to just be nominated as Best Actress?

The audition tomorrow could kick-start her new life. The one she was meant to be living. The one where she's applauded for her insightful portrayal of characters, where her films are critically and commercially acclaimed. The one where men will do anything for just one night – no, one full *minute* – in her company, and treat her with nothing but the utmost respect and dignity. The one where her peers are the famous faces that she now sees day in, day out in the newspapers and on television.

That life. The one that comes to mind when she gets *that* feeling. Where she's richer and more famous than she ever thought possible, where Kaylin never need worry about anything again.

Kaylin.

She checked herself, realising that she was getting carried away again. Kaylin was the reason she was doing this, but Kaylin was also the reason that she needed to be careful not to get over excited.

Things are different now. But it's up to me to make sure they stay that way.

The last thing she wanted was for things to go back to the way they were.

She allowed a small chuckle at this.

The way things were. It was only a few days ago!

But things had changed in the past few days. She definitely had, and Kaylin had been acting differently.

Kimberley pictured her only daughter's face from the other night, and shuddered. She looked so much like her father, but yet she knew that wasn't the only reason it haunted her.

It was the pure anger, and the hardness that she didn't know had existed in Kaylin until that moment. Somehow, paradoxically, her eyes had been cold and emotionless, yet also seething with absolute rage.

Kimberley had never seen a stare like that before. Not in a reality, not in a film, and certainly not on the face of her own child.

Her mind drifted to her ex-husband again. He was coming to mind a lot recently, and it wasn't helped by the fact that as Kaylin was getting older she was beginning to look more and more like him.

There was no doubt in her mind as to the identity of Kaylin's father. Well, not anymore at least.

She definitely looked nothing like the other one. The lying casting director who got what he wanted and then reneged on the promises he'd made.

Bastard...

She shook the thought out of her head, not wanting to remember him.

Kimberley looked towards Kaylin's room and her thoughts returned to her daughter's face. She'd inherited some of Kimberley's features, physical anyway.

Kimberley though about her own face, and gently reached her fingers up to touch the swollen part of her cheek. It still hurt, but it was better than it had been. It looked disgusting, she was under no illusions about that, but she hoped the man at the audition tomorrow would overlook it. They weren't going to start filming until the new year anyway. Although technically that was only about a week away.

The new year... The perfect time for a new start.

She reassured herself that this year would be better. She was going to make sure that Kaylin would be happier, and that she would be happier too.

I can be an actress and a mother. Why not? Other people do it.

Again, *actress* came before *mother*. And again, she didn't register the significance.

She shifted her position so that her feet were up on the sofa now. Yawning, she stretched her arms up in the air. She felt tired but didn't want to sleep. For the first time in months she actually wanted to live in the present, and enjoy the feeling of being relaxed and in control of her own destiny.

She looked around the flat as though for the first time.

The place wasn't that bad. She half sat, half lay facing the television and the front door. Kaylin's bedroom was behind her now, and hers was directly next to it.

She looked left to the kitchen, and right to the bathroom. She scanned the flat, moving her head slowly as though trying to memorise every detail. Ok, it wasn't a palace, and it could do with a spring clean, but she wasn't doing that badly. At least she and Kaylin had a roof over their heads, at least they weren't in the gutter.

Her attention was suddenly drawn to the front door, and she snapped her head sharply towards it, staring as though trying to solve a riddle. As though someone had repainted the door or changed the handle, and just not told her.

Something felt odd. A strange sense of unease crawled up her spine.

By sight, she double-checked that the door was both locked and bolted, but something definitely wasn't right.

She squinted in an attempt to sharpen her focus on the door and locate the source of her sudden apprehension.

Satisfied there was nothing wrong with the door, she sat up slightly, and began looking around the flat again. Searching for any threats, listening for any strange noises.

But there was nothing.

She turned and looked in the bedrooms, then again towards the kitchen and bathroom, as if the threat would reveal itself. When it didn't, she cautiously lay back on the sofa. After a couple of minutes she yawned again.

Maybe she just needed to rest. It'd been a while since she'd slept well. Not that her sleep had ever been particularly restful, but recently it'd been worse than it had for a long time. She couldn't get comfortable anymore. Every night the mattress was filled with rusty nails, the sheets fashioned from sandpaper.

Surrounded by silence, and ready for the warm embrace of restful sleep, she closed her eyes.

A few seconds later she snapped them open again.

There was... *something*.

And whatever it was bothered her on some deep, primal level. Her heartbeat had got faster, and she felt a wave of the purest fear sweeping through her body, forcing her bolt upright.

She stood and, on shaky legs, rushed to the kitchen. She grabbed the handle of the cutlery drawer and whipped it towards her. Reaching in, she pulled out the biggest knife from the drawer - a huge rusty thing with a rotten wooden handle. It had been in the flat when she'd moved in. She'd never actually used it, and didn't know why she hadn't just thrown it away, but right now she was grateful she hadn't.

She walked – no, *stalked* – back into the living room. Legs still shaking, breath becoming shallow.

Every sense was heightened; she was in a state of hypervigilance to an almost painful extent. She could hear *everything*, see *everything*. So why couldn't she find the source of her anxiety?

She creeped towards the bathroom, shifting her weight as she stepped to avoid the floorboards that she knew would creak. She'd had enough practice doing that during endless hours of sneaking around at night so that Kaylin wouldn't hear.

She got to the door, rushed in, and swung clumsily to the left positioning herself so she had a full view of the bath. She'd seen enough films to know how easily a person could hide in a bathtub, she wasn't about to risk getting stuck in this cramped room with –

With who exactly?

She didn't know. What she did know was that no matter who it was, they weren't in the bath.

She came out of the bathroom and swung sharply to the left, as though she might catch a glimpse of someone in her bedroom. From her vantage point at the doorway she couldn't see anything, although that didn't mean there was nobody there.

She inched inside, stepping carefully and deliberately. Always remembering to avoid the creaking floorboards. Kimberley could be as silent as the grave when she needed to be.

Don't say grave...

There was no-one inside. And there weren't exactly many hiding places where a person could be crouching or lying either.

Only one room left.

Kimberley - knife in left hand, muscles tensed in right - did not share Kaylin's rage. She'd been angry in her life of course, and she knew she would be again, but she didn't have that *rage*. Yet again, her mind flashed back to Kaylin's face the day after she'd acquired her bruise. That face was Robert through and through.

The mention of her ex-husband's name – even though not spoken aloud - stunned her for a second. She was accustomed to saying "my ex-husband", even in her own head.

Actually speaking his name, even only mentally, made him seem more present.

She shook herself back into the real world. She couldn't afford to be preoccupied, not now.

Out of nowhere panic tightened its grip. What had been a vague and fluctuating sensation now became tangible.

Kimberley defiantly turned around to her daughter's bedroom door and kicked it open. It slammed hard against the wardrobe door and bounced back, almost closing itself again.

Does something not want me to open this door?

Tough.

Kimberley shoulder barged into the door and pushed herself into her daughter's room like a rugby player. Her fear had reached a peak. It was life or death now. Him or me.

But there was nothing.

Again.

What the... How can there be nobody here? What is wrong with me?

What Kimberley didn't know was that earlier in the day her mind had picked up on something which only now was rising to her conscious mind, manifesting itself as fear. Fear which she wrongly attributed to the sense of an intruder.

There was something in the way that man was talking.

Joe. Joe Cameron.

As much as she felt she was being calm about this audition, she wasn't. If she'd been looking at it from a truly objective viewpoint, she would've wondered at the time just why he was so eager to meet with her, an actress with not many credits to her name and who he suddenly though would be perfect for an upcoming role.

And why had he said things in such an odd way?

Why did he keep saying he'd make it count? What did that even mean?

The problem for Kimberley was that none of these questions had occurred to her, because yet again she hadn't been objective. She'd been ##excited#, as always. She'd got *that* feeling. Eternity was waiting for her, who cared what words it was using to beckon her?

But now the residual fear of her unconscious questions had arrived in a mysterious wave, sending her into a panic in her own flat. She was scared with no idea why.

In a more lucid moment she might have wondered whether she had changed at all. Whether she was even capable of it anymore.

Back in the not-so-lucid moment, Kimberley Bellos stood in her flat holding a knife with a rusty blade and a mouldy wooden handle, and feeling a sick, fearful sensation that she hadn't felt in a long time.

She stood there for a full minute as the fear dissipated, seemingly knowing there was no need for it to exist here. Then the absurdity of the situation hit her.

She spoke to herself – aloud this time - like a mother talking to an overexcited toddler.

"Everything is ok, Kim. Put the knife away and stop being so jumpy. I have checked the flat. Everything is ok. Nothing is wrong. I just need to sleep. I need *a lot* of sleep!"

She gave another chuckle - this time from a combination of nerves and a slight feeling of embarrassment at speaking aloud to herself.

She began to feel a relief that she was merely overtired. Maybe a bit emotional, but nothing else. Certainly nothing to be worried about.

She strolled to the kitchen and put the knife back in the drawer, pretending to herself that her hands weren't still shaking.

She went past the sofa and lay down in the security of her bedroom this time, secretly wishing she that there was a lock on the door. She'd get that fixed as soon as she could. If she had a man around the house – a *real* man, not one of the others – he'd put up a bolt in no time.

She closed her eyes and hoped that sleep would take her soon, totally oblivious to the fact that she was in danger.

Something was going to happen.

But not here.

Not yet.

Twenty Six

Kaylin and the rest of her class were sat in their history lesson.

She loved this class for two reasons, firstly because she got to sit next to Anni, and secondly because she genuinely loved learning about the past. It was one of the few subjects that she got excited about.

It interested her how, in spite of all that has happened throughout history – the wars, the fights, the bloodshed - nothing has ever changed. Nobody ever seemed to learn anything, they just repeated old, destructive patterns over and over again.

She'd always found that fact curiously amusing. It meant a thousand years from now the same types of people would be having the same types of fights about the same types of things. Nothing would change.

It reminded slightly of her mum's life, and also, weirdly, her own.

She especially loved learning about the life stories of the major historical figures. It was interesting to see where they came from, and what turned them from normal people into the extraordinary ones that they would later become. She always thought there must have been something, or some *things*, in a person's life which would explain why they became so important in the history books. Not that it mattered really. It was always too late to stop them by the time anyone found out what they'd become anyway.

Kaylin was brought back to reality by the sound of Anni laughing. She was on top form today, making joke after joke and cracking up the rest of the class. Their teacher was a man named Mr. Nicholas, a pretty boy with high cheekbones and floppy hair. He looked to Kaylin like he'd fallen into teaching after the boy band had split up. He had a permanent cough and regularly paused mid-sentence to clear his throat, which gave ample opportunity for the more creative students – like Anni - to finish his sentences for him. And she was in her element today.

"The first world war, called the Great War, is the main reason..."

"That I look like a girl," she mumbled to Kay and the others sitting around her, causing an eruption of laughter from that side of the class.

Mr Nicholas, blissfully oblivious to the joke at his expense, continued.

"There were many causes, but the main trigger for the war is thought to be..."

"Located in my cheek-dimples," she said slightly louder so a few more of the class could hear.

Mr. Nicholas gave one of his *Disapproving Teacher* glares. He'd got quite good at those, as most teachers have to, although his own particular brand of frown always seemed to be slightly tinged with amusement. He appeared to be in on the joke in some way, as though they were all acting their roles and he was glaring at The Students because that's what he was obliged to do as The Teacher.

Anni and Kay looked at him, then at each other, and grinned. Anni had always made her friend laugh, even when Kaylin had felt like everything else in her life was falling apart. And she had lost count of the times she had felt like that.

Today she was feeling slightly more positive though. Her mum had seemed different for the first time in a long time, maybe history wouldn't repeat itself for once.

(Of course it will...)

Kay twitched her head slightly in an attempt to shake the voice away. She froze, sitting perfectly still and using her peripheral vision to ascertain whether anybody had turned towards her, or whether they were exhibiting any other signs that they had noticed. They hadn't, but she needed to be careful. People who twitch their heads at nothing are generally not very popular at school.

She exhaled deeply.

Hand-outs started being passed around the class. That was another thing Kaylin liked about Anni, whenever she wasn't at school Anni would pick up extra handouts for her. And on the occasions when she'd been too upset to do her homework, Anni had actually completed it for her. The two girls were so similar in their work that they even made the same mistakes, so the teachers could never accuse Anni of doing Kay's work - or vice versa - because there was no way of telling. One time their English teacher had accused the two girls of cheating after they'd sat a test and achieved almost identical results. The next day Kay was put in one room, Anni in another, and they were both made to complete a new test.

They both got seventy-two out of eighty, and they'd got almost exactly the same questions wrong too.

The girls loved that story, it made them both feel they were that much closer to each other. As Anni had excitedly told her parents at the time, "Even sisters don't get the same test results!"

The class were busy studying the handouts. In spite of that ever-present voice, Kaylin really did feel better today. Even if things did eventually go back to the way there were, at least her mum was trying. At least she was making the effort to be different.

She just hoped her mum would try for a bit longer this time.

Hope.

There was that word again, that beast again.

(And how long will she change for this time?)

Kaylin didn't snap her head this time, instead she fought back.

I don't care.

(That's not true. She'll go back to being the same way in a few days.)

Not necessarily.

(Not unless she gets famous. And what are the chances of that?)

The fight in Kaylin took a knock at that. It was true. The only way her mum would be satisfied and normal –

whatever that meant – would be if she did get famous, then she'd stop being depressed all the time.

(But she won't get famous. So you know what you have to do.)

Kaylin felt nauseous, her stomach tightened and her throat suddenly felt as though it was coated with a thick liquid.

What do I have to do?

(You know.)

No I don't.

(Yes you do. You know it Kaylin.)

And she did. Of course she did.

I'm not doing that.

(You might have to. Save her from all the pain. Put-)

No...

(Her-)

No...

(Down.)

"No!"

Annika turned to face Kaylin.

"Oh, come on," she motioned to the hand-out, "its three questions Kay! I think we'll be ok!"

Kaylin snapped back to reality in a heartbeat.

"Is it only three?"

She looked at the paper in front of her.

"Oh yeah, oh, I suppose we can do it. Well, I can anyway, I don't know about you. You'll probably write 'cheek-dimples' all over the page!"

Kaylin surprised herself at how quickly she could go from one extreme to the other. From silent self-imposed torture to happy teenager again.

For not the first time, and definitely not the last, she thought she'd probably make a pretty good actress. And she hoped – desperately – that her mum would too.

In fact her very last shred of hope was counting on it.

Twenty Seven

Nothing much happened that evening.

Kaylin got home from school, and Kimberley made dinner. It was really just another night in the flat for mother and daughter.

They ate and spoke a bit about their days – Kimberley didn't mention her scare, and Kaylin didn't mention the voice. They watched television, and went to bed.

Kaylin thought about school, Kimberley thought about her audition.

In the years to come Kaylin would replay this night, scouring her mind, hunting for some clue, searching for some omen. Trying to isolate a particular moment or word spoken as a sign of what was to come. As a warning that she should have heeded.

But there was nothing.

It was just another night.

Quiet.

Calm.

Life gives no warnings.

Twenty Eight

Kimberley's alarm had barely started ringing before her hand shot out and silenced it.

It hadn't been a good night's sleep. She'd been fine until she'd actually got into bed, when it dawned on her that the only thing between her and her big break was those few hours of sleep.

It'd then taken an hour of talking herself out of heart palpitations and shallow breaths until she'd felt calm – or the closest approximation she could get to it - in order to be able to sleep.

Even then, she hadn't slept for long. Somewhere in her mind, an internal alarm woke her every hour or so with thoughts of the future.

She lay in bed and rubbed her tired, red eyes, flinching as she touched her bruise. She yawned, and abruptly cut it short as her facial muscles stretched the sensitive nerve endings on the swollen side of her face. She must have slept on that side of her face, as yawning hadn't hurt the day before.

She began to wonder whether she should even bother with the audition after all this. She was tired and she looked terrible, and what if she got stood up again? How much more rejection could she realistically take at this point?

What Kimberley didn't know, what she would never know, is that she didn't get stood up the other day because of her bruise. She didn't actually get stood up at all, she'd simply got too excited and written down the wrong place to meet.

She blamed the bruise though and wondered if that was a valid enough reason to stay home. At times like this, any reason had to be what Kimberley would consider to be a valid one. She couldn't cancel an audition or meeting merely because she was nervous, or for fear of rejection, but she *could* cancel if she thought there was a genuine reason she was wasting her time.

Creative people never want to cancel anything just in case they miss their break.

Unless they have a *valid reason...*

She began wondering if the bruise would suffice. Was it a good enough excuse – no, not excuse, *reason* - to get her off the hook, to allow her to stay here in bed, in her normal life, and not have to possibly cope with the rejection, or even cope with the success and whatever unknowns that might bring?

But what if this was her big break? How would she handle the fame, the success? What if it wasn't all it was cracked up to be? What if she would be even unhappier as a famous actress than as an unemployed one?

What if. That game again.

Another reason flashed through her mind.

Kaylin.

It was Saturday, maybe she should spend the day with her daughter and make up for the last few days. Kaylin would love that, it'd make her happy. Kimberley could even pretend to be a good mum for a while.

Kimberley had been to enough auditions to realise that this was just the nerves talking. There was no *valid reason* to cancel.

She would go to the audition because her whole life had revolved around becoming an actress. If she faltered now, at what could well be the last hurdle, then what had been the point in everything that had come before? She needed fame if only to validate her entire life up to this point.

It was all a waste otherwise.

She would go to the audition, and then she would spend time with Kaylin tomorrow, or next week. It was settled.

And with that, the butterflies in her stomach started, and in her mind the same four words repeated like a mantra.

This might be it.

And if this audition was her big break then she and Kaylin wouldn't need to worry about money or each other - or *anything* - for a long time.

She still felt the slight apprehension from the day before, but it mixed with excitement now. And after all, this one felt different.

It felt like one of the special ones.

No, she had to go to the audition. She would go.

Years from now, this might be the story she'd be telling an acting class to help them go out and be brave and follow their own dreams.

She looked at the time. It was eleven o'clock.

She was meeting Joe Cameron in Old Street at 1pm, which gave her just enough time to shower, eat and cover the bruise with makeup.

She'd informed him about the bruise the day before and he didn't seem to mind, telling her that it was, "amazing what we can do with makeup". That's when he mentioned they weren't shooting for a week or so anyway, so it would've likely gone down a lot by then.

If she got the part.

She *had* to get the part...

Please...

With that the entire house of cards came tumbling down, and she realised that she was as excited and nervous and desperate as she always was. She could lie to Kaylin, but not to herself. She wanted this, and not just so that she could take care of Kaylin. She wanted it to satisfy *that* feeling. To feed the addiction that roared through her veins like an express train.

It was vengeance and it was proof. Revenge for all the bad things everybody had said to her and done to her, and proof that that she was worthwhile, that she was – *is* – exceptional.

Proof that Kimberley Bellos is not a failure.

Ok, so the marriage didn't last, but so what? Nobody cares about that when you're famous. Nobody cares about anything when you're famous, except pleasing you. They start asking – no, *begging* – you to be in their films, and the past doesn't matter anymore. Everything becomes prologue.

She had to get famous. Otherwise everything up to this point was in vain. All the struggling and problems, the fact that she wasn't much of a mother, that she would probably never be much of a wife. Fame would validate her and everything she'd done and been and thought and felt.

It doesn't matter when you're famous. As long as the audiences love you, acceptance is guaranteed.

The excitement was getting too much, and she felt slightly nauseous. She took a long, deep breath in through her nose for a count of three, and exhaled slowly and deeply through her mouth for a count of five – a technique she'd learned from an acting class. She did this ten times and then, feeling slightly light-headed, got out of bed and began getting ready.

***

Kaylin was woken by the sound of the shower.

After procrastinating for a while, she wrenched herself out of bed and threw on some clothes. It was Saturday so it wasn't like she had to be anywhere.

She ambled into the kitchen, sleepy-eyed and overtired, just as her mum was making tea.

"Morning mum."

Kimberley had her back to her and seemed to be mumbling. She was pouring hot water into her cup, and apparently talking to it.

Kaylin watched as she turned and took a teabag from the white tin on the counter, grimacing as though the tin was filled with slugs, then beaming as though the love of her life had just walked in. All the while she was muttering to herself, and totally oblivious to her daughter.

Kaylin wasn't worried, she'd seen all this before.

"Mum..." Kaylin said, softly putting her hand on her mum's shoulder.

Kimberley jumped as though woken from a deep sleep.

"Kay! You scared the life out of me," she said, laughing but obviously shaken.

"Sorry, I just wanted to say good morning and good luck."

"I know, sorry Kay! I was just going over my audition pieces in case they ask to hear them today. Do you want some tea?"

Kaylin shook her head, she never could eat or drink much in the morning. Until she'd managed to fully prise her eyes open, she never wanted anything - other than more sleep.

"So, are you ready to meet that man?"

"Sort of. I will be by the time I get there."

"Are you sure he's ok, mum? I mean, that man on the news..."

"Oh Kaylin, none of those girls were anything like me. They were all younger and naive. *And* another actress I know worked with this man once, so he's harmless. He's a professional Kay, don't worry."

That smelled like a lie to Kaylin, but she let it go. She had got to the point where she could pretty reliably tell when her mum was lying. It wasn't like her mum was being malicious either. She probably thought there was no point in worrying Kaylin, which is why she'd pretended she'd checked out the man she was going to meet.

"Ok, mum," Kaylin said.

Her mum started mumbling her audition monologues again, and Kaylin started playing with the magnets on the fridge.

The magnets were odd. There were only two of them, and they'd both been free inside cereal boxes. One was a cheerful orange elephant wearing a blue Fez, winking playfully at Kaylin, as it had done for the past few years. It was one of those expressions that looked harmless at first, then slowly got creepier and creepier the longer you looked at it.

The other magnet looked like some kind of hut with a rainbow coming out of the roof, although she'd never been clear about what it was actually supposed to be. And she'd always wondered what the link was supposed to be too. What has a hut with a rainbow got to do with breakfast cereal? Not that the elephant suggested fine dining, but at least it looked like maybe it liked to eat the product it came with.

A new thought broke in, unannounced and uninvited.

(He fucked her then he fucked up her face and you did nothing.)

Kaylin hesitated for only a second, swallowing down the shock and hurt to spare her mum. She continued playing with the magnets, and fought to resist the urge to look again at her mum's swollen face.

(You should get the address.)

Leave me alone...

(Get the address Kaylin.)

Stop this. Please...

(Get the fucking address.)

Which...? What address?

(Which address do you think? The address of the place she's going to.)

Why?

(So you know where she is. So if anything happens you can go there and do what needs to be done. Its time you started protecting her. She can't do it herself. You have to.)

No. It's not that man, it can't be. Nothing's going to happen. Stop this. Things are ok now.

Her hands shifted the magnets faster and faster across the fridge door, as though they were being chased by some unseen aggressor and she was moving them out of harm's way. She knocked the elephant and it fell to the ground. Kimberley turned at the noise as Kaylin stood staring at the elephant, winking at her from the kitchen floor.

(Don't you want to protect her? What if she DIES Kaylin? WHAT IF YOUR MUM ACTUALLY DIES?)

Kaylin jerked her head, sending a bolt of pain through her neck and down her spine.

Her mum eyed her with a look somewhere between concern and annoyance.

"Kay? Are you ok?"

Kaylin bent down and picked up the magnet, slowly placing it back on the fridge as she scoured her mind for an explanation.

"Yeah mum, I'm fine. My neck's a bit... stiff. It feels better when I do that."

She was normally more convincing than this, for some reason today the words actually *felt* like lies in her mouth. Not that Kimberley pursued it.

She turned back around, facing away from Kaylin, and took another sip of tea.

Silence for a few moments, and then Kimberley went back to mouthing one of her monologues. Kaylin continued playing with the magnets. The voice seemed to have left for the moment, but she knew it'd be back.

Kaylin wanted to occupy her mind, keep busy.

"So, er... do you feel ok about the audition mum? Do you think you'll break a leg and everything?"

She gave a feeble laugh.

"Mmm? Yes," her mum responded.

Silence again.

"Can I help with anything? Shall I help you go over the lines or something?"

Kimberley still stood with her back to Kaylin.

"No," she said quickly. "But thanks Kay."

"What if you do the speech for me and I can tell you what I think? I can be your audience mum!"

"Kay."

There was a slight harshness in her mum's voice now as she turned to face Kaylin.

"Could you... I just need to go over this before I go in a minute. Thanks for offering but I just need quiet to do this. Ok?"

Kaylin deflated slightly at this.

I knew nothing would change. I knew it.

Kaylin felt her stomach tense. The voice returned.

(People never change. The only way to help them is to free them from themselves. They can't choose to change, they have to be forced.)

That's not right! She can change. She will.

(No, she will not. You have to change her.)

I can't change her! How am I supposed to do that?!

(You know how.)

An image flashed into Kaylin's mind. Her mum in a cell, a gunshot. Blood.

So much blood.

No! Please! I'm not going to –

(You should. It's for her own good. Why let her suffer? She'll be back here tonight crying and upset, back inviting more men over. She won't stop herself. You have to.)

NO! I won't. I'd rather have her in tears than not at all. That's enough now. Stop!

(Would you really? Would you honestly rather have her in tears? In pain? Do you think she's happy? Look at her.)

No.

(Look. At. Her.)

Kaylin looked from the fridge magnets to her mother. She no longer had her back to Kaylin, but was in profile. Her eyes were closed and she was mouthing something into her cup, occasionally gesticulating and changing facial expression.

(She looks bruised and pathetic.)

Something inside Kaylin could not fight that time, or didn't want to. She had to agree. It was true. Her mum was bruised, and did look pathetic.

And nothing had changed either.

She walked out of the kitchen, closing the door when she got to her room as if trying to shut out her mum and the whole situation. She lay down on her bed.

To her horror, she began to realise that she'd left the kitchen because she was scared about what might happen if she'd stayed there. Scared of what she might do.

She closed her eyes and the tears began. Slowly at first, then coursing down the sides of her face and onto her pillow.

A few minutes later her mum called out.

"Bye Kay. I'll be back at about three probably. This is it for us! Wish me luck!"

The door slammed shut before Kaylin had a chance to open her mouth.

She sighed that big sigh again and rested her hands behind her head as she stared up at the ceiling. She felt like she didn't know anything anymore.

What was happening to her?

In the kitchen she'd felt...impulses that were never there before. Was she really scared someone would hurt her mum?

Or was she scared that she might do something herself?

She didn't want to be alone with these thoughts. Her mind needed to be kept busy, occupied.

She decided to go into the front room and watch the news. Something new might have happened with that killer. If he'd been caught maybe she could stop worrying so much. And it would be good to catch up on the news anyway, Anni always did and she seemed to know everything that was going on.

She flicked on the TV, the background noise a welcome relief and immediately causing her to feel less alone.

It took a full minute before her mind drifted back to that voice, and what it had said. What she had said.

She didn't want that voice to ever come back. But whether it did or not, she was left reeling from the fact that she could ever have thought those things, and so calmly. How could she think such sick things and contemplate... such horrors? The arguing the points back and forth as though if it was of no consequence what she chose to do.

Her thoughts were interrupted by the doorbell. It startled her at first, but maybe her mum had decided to just come back home and forget the audition. Maybe things had changed.

Or maybe she just forgot her travelcard or her keys or something.

She wiped her eyes, walked over and unlocked the door. As she pulled it open she fixed a smile to her face, ready to play the obedient daughter role again.

The smile disappeared and her mouth dropped open at the person standing in front of her. He was immaculately dressed, as though ready for an important meeting at the office.

"Hello Kay," said Annika's dad. "Can I come in?"

Twenty Nine

Old Street underground station sits between the Northern Line tube stations of Angel and Moorgate. It lies beneath the central island of a huge roundabout, which itself is a curious hybrid of cement, trees and industrial sized dustbins, thrown together and placed in the centre of the hectic roads which swirl around it. The tornado of metal and rubber never quite engulfing the eye at its centre.

The eight main entrances to the station are located at varying points around the outside of the roundabout, sloping tunnels connecting the world above to the subterranean heart of Old Street. These pathways are the only indication that a station exists there at all – the words *underground station* never being so apt.

Not many people are aware that there is actually a ninth exit hidden behind a small, unmarked doorway in the ticket hall, which leads directly to the centre of the roundabout's island. Here, next to the dustbins and parked cars, and nestled under a handful of small trees, sits an old park bench. A haven of sorts, a place to see but not be seen, hidden by trees and bushes and concrete blocks. A safe place to sit and watch the world go by, behind camouflage. Every so often a driver or passenger in one of the circling vehicles may get a glimpse of someone – usually alone - sitting on the bench on the island. Just a quick look, a flash. Enough to think something has been seen but not enough to know whether the ghost was real or a figment of an overactive imagination.

On any given day, what they saw probably was a real person sitting there, staring out. Watching the commuters, the tourists, and, as day turns to evening turns to night, the drunken revellers and night owls.

At every audition in Old Street that Kimberley had ever been to, she had sat there beforehand. Dreaming of the new life of which the upcoming audition will be a gateway. The pathway as hidden – but as real – as the route to the station itself.

Like a pre-game ritual, she would sit still and prepare herself. Get ready to go in to the room and show them just what she can do. Who she is, and who she could be for them.

But she wasn't sitting there today.

She'd arrived at the station at exactly 12.45pm and headed straight for Exit Three, the closest exit for the studios she needed to get to. There was no time to sit and stare, no time to dream.

The future was waiting, she needed to grab it with both hands.

She was feeling more pleased with herself today than she had for a long time. She'd woken up, gone over some audition pieces and got ready in good time. The make-up job she'd done on herself looked pretty good too. There was still swelling and slight discolouration, but she looked enough like herself to feel satisfied. And, more importantly, to not feel overly self-conscious.

On top of all that she'd arrived exactly fifteen minutes before the audition, which she'd always said was the perfect length of time before a performance. Any earlier and she'd look too keen, and give herself time to be nervous and begin doubting herself. Any later and she'd look like she didn't want the part enough.

No, fifteen minutes was perfect.

The studios were housed in an old building a few minutes' walk from the station. It looked like it was once some kind of exclusive property – maybe high end offices or possibly even luxury apartments - albeit one that somebody had left to rot.

There was an air of crumbled elegance about it - a wedding dress in the attic, decayed and mouldy, its splendour a distant memory.

This didn't particularly surprise Kimberley, she'd learnt early on that television and film were all about image. Nothing mattered but the end result and the look of the image projected on the screen. She'd once taken on a role in a short film which was filmed in its entirety inside what looked like an old barn. The place was dilapidated - hay still strewn about the floor, dust and grime covering the walls, and a particularly nasty smell hanging in the rank air. A literal pigsty, all except for the area which was to be filmed. A flimsy-looking set comprising three plasterboard walls and a bank of cameras facing them. The area was immaculate, decorated to look like the dining room of a fine Edwardian country house. When she eventually saw the finished cut of the film it looked stunning, as if filmed in a perfectly restored mansion, rather than a dank and dingy barn with a leaking roof and the ever-present smell of rotting animal dung.

She walked to the small doorway of the building which she assumed must be the front entrance. Her eyes scanned the list of names scrawled beside the intercom system, which looked in as bad a state as the rest of the building. All the names were faded, although oddly there seemed to be only one button to press anyway.

She pushed it, admiring the results of her do-it-yourself manicure on her fingers, and stood waiting for someone to respond.

For a moment she thought she heard a crackle, but then there was nothing for a few seconds.

She pressed it again, holding the button down longer this time, more from nerves than impatience. Her left foot began involuntarily tapping on the floor.

She waited. Nothing.

She leaned towards the intercom and squinted at the list trying to make out the names when a voice loudly crackled from the speaker.

She jumped.

"Hello?" the robotic voice said.

"Hello. My names Kimberley. I'm here for the audition?"

"Kimberley? One second..."

There was a sound of papers rustling. Kimberley felt that familiar mix of nerves and excitement.

"Yup. Here you are. Come right in, please. We're in the basement."

She attempted to thank the voice but was cut off by the loud buzz and snap of the door being unlocked remotely. She slowly pushed open the door - which to her surprise didn't creak much - and walked through the crumbling doorframe.

Directly opposite the door a piece of white paper had been taped to the wall. Whoever put it there hadn't needed to worry about the tape marking the paint as most of it had already peeled off, peppering the grungy brown carpet with white-yellow flakes. The paper was stuck above the top of the stairs, and had the word 'Audition' written in the centre in thick blue marker. Underneath this there was a crudely-drawn arrow, pointing down the stairs.

No expense spared, huh?

Kimberley began the pep talk she always recited before going into an audition.

Be calm, just relax, they want me to be good. They want me to be the one they're looking for. I can do this. Be calm, just relax, they want me to be good. They want me to be the one they're looking for. I can do this. Be calm, just relax, they...

She was on the brink of eternity again, her mind swimming with images of fame and success. Awards ceremonies, beautiful houses, amazing cars, Kaylin sipping a cocktail - non-alcoholic, of course - while lying by their luxury pool. Luxury #heated# pool.

It could all be mine. And Kaylin's.

Be calm, just relax, they want me to be good. They want me to be the one they're looking for. I can do this.

I. Can. Do. This.

She inhaled deeply and began walking down the steep, narrow stairs, all the while struggling to remember the first lines of her monologues. She remembered one of her acting teachers – a curious woman who insisted on being called Lady O – and how she had always told the students to only focus on the first line as they walked onstage, and not to try and hold the entire speech in their heads. Kimberley could hear her voice now, addressing the class in that odd and never quite identifiable accent.

"Everythink it vill flow from de ferz line."

Kimberley liked Lady O, she had been her first acting teacher and always seemed to give the young actress extra support and advice. She'd taken her under her wing, and Kimberley had never known why she'd been singled out for special treatment when none of the others students had. Not that she wasn't grateful for it, she needed all the help she could get.

In many ways, she still did.

As Kimberley walked down the stairs she could see that the rest of the building was probably going to take its lead in décor from the upstairs. More peeling paint and dirty carpets, although at Kimberley's career level, most of the places seemed to look like this. Some had looked even worse. At least the air wasn't thick with the smell of animal waste.

She allowed herself a brief smile at this. A bittersweet smile, as maybe this wasn't the one in a million audition she'd thought it would be. Maybe this one wouldn't be so different from the others after all.

She quickly squashed the negative thoughts and tried to instead focus on only positive ones.

She repeated her mantra again. The words felt slightly hollower this time.

She held onto the hope that she would reach the bottom of the stairs and see a pure white backdrop, with dazzling lights pointed directly at it. Crew members would be standing around and fiddling with cameras, holding those long microphones which she seemed to remember were called booms. One or two important people would be sitting at a table facing the backdrop, sipping sparkling water from frosted glasses, and waiting to be impressed by the next hopeful. There'd be the faint smell of cigarette smoke in the air coming from the clothes of both the assembled crew and each of the auditionees who had already had their shot.

She felt that irresistible mix of excitement and nerves again, but it soon disappeared when she reached the bottom of the stairs.

It was a basement. An *empty* basement.

Totally barren, and seemingly stripped of everything but the flooring and a single metal fold-up chair. The office-style strip lighting was on – she could her it humming overhead - but that was the only sign of life as far as she could see.

"Hello?"

No answer.

Even the forced enthusiasm Kimberley had tried to muster on seeing the basement dissipated into nothingness now. She wasn't scared as most of the auditions she'd been to had been disorganised and at least a bit strange, a lot of the time it just went with the territory. There was no fear, just disappointment and confusion.

The only possible hope was the blue door she noticed on the other side of the room. Even from where she stood, she could see it looked dense, strong. Probably a fire door.

It looked heavy, as though made from the most solid of wood, and there was a glass porthole just above its centre. The glass was also tough, she noticed it had thin metal criss-crossing through it, as though to prevent it from shattering in the event it was struck.

There seemed to be a faint light coming from behind the glass. Kimberley walked over to it, hoping that this would be where the audition would be held. Hoping that she wasn't just wasting her time.

Out of nowhere she suddenly began to feel uneasy, but couldn't work out why. Her mind flashed back to the day before, at home with the knife. The emotion felt identical, which was odd as what could possibly exit both here and at home that would elicit such a specific response?

The floorboards creaked under her feet as she walked. The sound of each one mocked her as she stepped, echoing off the barren surfaces in the room, playfully reminding her that she was alone. Reminding her that nobody else was around.

It was just her.

That's when she realised *why* she felt uneasy.

The whole place was too quiet. If there are crew members around, why aren't they making noise? Where are the people who have just been auditioned? Or the ones about to be auditioned?

She decided that if nobody was standing on the other side of the door, or if she didn't at least see a sign telling her where to go, then she would leave. Fame and fortune could start another day, this was starting to get creepy.

She walked slowly over to the door. Somewhere in her mind she registered that she didn't want to get to the door quickly as, if she did after all find nobody there, she didn't actually want to leave. There was a chance – albeit a miniscule one – that this could still be her big break, she didn't want to leave just because she'd got all scared of an empty room and some floorboards creaking. She'd felt scared yesterday and nothing had actually been wrong, so why should she trust the emotion now?

She got to the door and tiptoed in order to peer through the porthole.

She found herself staring down a long corridor, which got darker as it stretched away from her meaning she couldn't see what was at the other end. She tried the handle but the door was locked, and felt as dense and strong as she had suspected.

She squinted through the glass and into the nothingness. There was something at the end, but she couldn't make out what it was.

She felt a flutter in her chest for as a moment as the object at the end of the corridor appeared to be a person standing perfectly still, although she couldn't be sure. She strained her eyes and forced them to focus on the figure at the end.

For all she knew, that figure was staring straight back at her.

She leaned forward until her head touched the cool glass of the porthole. She jumped at the feel of the cold, dead glass on her forehead, and realised how hot the basement had become.

She squinted her eyes again – what *was* that?

A sense of relief washed over her as she realised she wasn't looking at a person, but a stepladder which had been set up with clothes hanging off the rungs on both sides. The angle of it gave it a skeletal look, like a malnourished person whose clothes are hanging off.

She briefly wondered who would have taken the time to set up a stepladder and drape clothes on it, and then wondered why.

It struck her how much the legs of the ladder looked like some kind of metal skeleton, the bones of which were shining in the darkness.

And did the top – the head? - just move?

She focused on the top of the object, still squinting, trying to understand what she was seeing. Fear began creeping down her back. A disembodied hand, freezing each segment of her spine as the fingers walked themselves down.

Her mind knew she wasn't looking at a skeleton, at some long dead person draped in a shroud, staring back at her with soulless eyes. But her body's physiology was telling her that it wasn't so sure.

And did the part near the top – the face? – just turn towards her?

Her calves began hurting as she'd been on tiptoes for so long, but she didn't drop down. She stood and stared through the glass, so intrigued as to what she was looking at down the end of the corridor that she couldn't have moved even if she'd wanted to.

She suddenly began to feel that she would want to move very soon.

She was so busy looking through the glass that she didn't notice the footsteps behind her.

Careful footsteps.

The footsteps of someone who knew which floorboards would creak and which ones would not.

The footsteps of who or whatever lived here.

Her gaze was totally focused on the object at the end of the corridor, and so she didn't notice the shadow appear on the floor. She didn't even notice when the shadow began creeping up the door as the figure behind her got closer.

And, two seconds later, she was struck so hard on the back of her head that it was too late for her to notice anything at all.

Thirty

"Would you like some tea?"

There was a slight tremble in Kaylin's voice as she spoke, which was no wonder as she was feeling an odd sensation that her feet were no longer planted on the ground.

Her best friend's dad was standing at her front door, uninvited and unannounced, wearing a demeanour that wouldn't have looked out of place at a funeral.

The question about the tea was nothing but a reflex, what else was she supposed to say? Asking about tea was what most adults would have said in the same situation, wouldn't they?

Kaylin thought so, and fell back on it as the correct response. A stock phrase, something familiar to reassure her that some things were still normal.

Although she got the feeling that this situation was far from normal.

"No thank you, Kaylin. Would it be alright for me to come in, please?"

Kaylin paused. She knew and liked Annika's dad very much, often wishing he was her own father. But his previous character wasn't outweighing the context of this meeting. Why hadn't he called? Had he waited for Kaylin's mum to leave before coming over?

If so, why?

Kaylin nodded slowly, then moved out of the doorway to let him pass. He walked in almost deferentially, wiping his feet on the mat and ensuring not to brush against Kaylin as he walked.

He stood by the sofa.

"Is it ok for me to sit down please Kaylin?"

"Um, yes. Sorry, we don't have many... visitors."

Well, that isn't entirely true...

Annika's Dad sat down at one end of the sofa and motioned for Kaylin to sit at the other. She hesitated.

"It's ok Kaylin," he said, smiling and gesturing to the sofa again, "please. Have a seat. Make yourself at home."

He tried laughing at his own joke but couldn't quite manage it.

Kaylin didn't even try to laugh. She noticed he was smartly dressed and carrying his briefcase – his 'work outfit' as Annika called it.

She felt a cold fear rising up inside her. It was though some horrendous chain of events had been set in motion, events which she would be completely powerless to stop. And there was no doubt in her mind that whatever was about to happen she would *desperately* want it to stop.

Annika!

"Is Annika ok? Did something happen?"

He raised a hand to reassure her.

"Annika's fine. Don't worry, she's fine."

He smiled again, which this time did relax Kaylin slightly. She always thought he had a kind smile, and it worked to give her some measure of comfort.

There was something in his body language and facial expressions which was... She couldn't quite place it, but something was off. She looked at him sitting on the sofa, composed and professional, but every so often scratching the back of his neck, or wiping some imaginary dirt from his suit. It took her a few moments to realise, but when she did it came as both a relief and a shock.

He was scared.

He noticed her watching him and gave another smile. Again, it radiated warmth and openness.

Although it probably has to because he's a psychiatrist. He needs to be able to put people at ease before telling them things they might not want to hear...

A silence hung between them. Annika's dad was wringing his hands now, as though working up to something he wasn't comfortable with.

He breathed in deeply, then released the breath slowly, his eyes closed all the while.

Then, he spoke.

"Kaylin," he began, "I'm not sure how to say this so I'll just be as honest and direct with you as I can. I hope that's ok?"

Kaylin nodded in spite of the terror that his words had just induced. What was happening here? She felt everything spinning out of her control – not that it ever was, but the illusion was suddenly and totally shattered.

She wanted to talk but knew that the words wouldn't come out. She felt they'd stick somewhere on the journey from her larynx to her lips, choking her. Asphyxiating her with her own fear.

Annika's dad spoke slowly and calmly.

"As you know, I'm a psychiatrist. Last week I treated a gentleman who'd been ordered to come and see me by a court. Sometimes a judge will order a person to have therapy for one reason or another. This man was an alcoholic and also used illegal drugs, and he had been caught driving under the influence of both. Due to his rapidly deteriorating health, among other mitigating factors – um, that just means other things that were taken into account that helped him – the court found it more just to order him to receive psychiatric help rather than be given a custodial sentence."

He stopped talking and looked down at his hands. His face all of a sudden seemed lined, as though he'd aged a hundred years since he'd come to the door. Kaylin felt tears welling in her eyes, and fought to keep herself from breaking down. This was so unnatural, so strange.

What is going on? Where's mum?

"Kaylin," he said, "that man... that man is... was, your father."

Each word fired into Kaylin like a barrage of arrows from a crossbow, each one piercing deeper than the last. The final one striking her square in the chest.

The words of the last few minutes ricocheted around her head.

My father?

How can that... What's he talking about?

"What do you mean?" she asked, the words seemingly coming from somewhere outside her body. Her voice had a horrible pleading tone, begging him for answers or an explanation or *something* to get the world spinning on its axis again.

"I know it's a shock Kaylin. Maybe we should just sit for a moment and you can have some time to take it all in. It's a lot to hear all at once."

Kaylin thought back to the story he'd told. He spoke about an alcoholic, addicted to illegal drugs. He'd said something about a court and a custodial sentence. And did he mention driving under the influence?

"I don't," she began. "None of this makes any sense..."

Mr. Nader inhaled sharply, as if about to speak, when something Kaylin had registered in her subconscious now came screaming into her conscious mind. She cut him short.

"What do you mean *was* my father?"

Doctor Mark Nader, renowned psychiatrist, acclaimed author of no less than thirty psychological papers, looked as though he no longer had the ability to speak English. It was as if his years of training and practice were mocking him as he floundered for the correct response.

"I mean..."

He looked down at his hands, and Kaylin noticed he abruptly stopped wringing them as if unaware he'd even been doing it at all. He rubbed his brow with the tips of his fingers, and seemed surprised to find his forehead slick with sweat.

His eyes scanned the room, as if looking for the words he needed.

"I mean..."

He didn't need to finish. Something welled up in Kaylin and she burst into tears. She knew what he was going to say, just like she knew why he'd used the past tense about her father.

The tears came fast and hard. Floods of tears for a father she'd never met and knew nothing about. She felt foolish for crying but couldn't stop.

How can I be sad? Why should I be? I never knew him.

But she was sad, she was devastated. Somewhere she'd hoped that one day maybe she'd meet him, that he'd marry her mum and they'd be a family and be happy and eat together and tell each other stories about their days and go on holidays and live in a house and open presents at Christmas and go to see uncles and meet cousins she didn't even know about and be just like Annika's family. That had all been immediately and cruelly taken away from her.

And the pain cut even deeper being delivered by a member of that family which she so wanted to emulate.

Mr. Nader reached over and took her hand.

"I'm so sorry Kaylin. I'm so sorry darling. I'm so sorry."

His voice broke slightly when he said the word 'darling', as though he himself were about to cry.

"Why did...? I mean, why?"

Her voice was pleading again. A newly widowed woman, begging the police at her door to make it different, to tell her it's all untrue – he's ok and he's coming home.

"Why what, Kaylin?"

His voice was gentle and soothing. The psychiatrist falling back on the skills familiar to him. As with Kaylin earlier, he apparently took comfort in the usual, the routine.

"Why are you telling me?"

Then, anger broke through. The tears stopped flowing and Kaylin became the warrior again. She noticed Annika's dad reeled back at the change in her, and he loosed his grip on her hand slightly as though the anger was somehow repelling him. She saw the terror in his eyes as her defences rose up defiantly and she screamed in his face.

"WHY ARE YOU TELLING ME?! I DIDN'T NEED TO KNOW!"

He was silent, as if both her words and the ferocity of them had stunned hm.

He was took him time to respond, as if weighing his words so as to ensure they were not the wrong ones.

"You did need to know Kaylin. I wish you didn't, but... Your father wanted me to talk to you. It was what he wished. I didn't want to have to come here and tell you any of this, Kaylin, but I had to. I'm so, so sorry."

"You're sorry? Well so am I! Look at me, I've been sorry my whole life and now it's even worse! Look what you've done to me! Get out! Just get..."

The defences collapsed as quickly as they'd amassed, giving way to more tears as Kaylin broke down again. She still felt a powerful, insistent anger, but realised she was no longer directing it at Mr. Nader, or at her father, or at anyone else in the world. She was directing it at herself.

(Why are you crying? You didn't even know him.)

He was my father!

(When? When was he your father? When was the last time he saw you? Did you get to call him Daddy, Kaylin? Did he ever even come to see you? So what have you lost Kaylin? What exactly have you lo-)

"Hope!" Kaylin screamed aloud. "There's no hope anymore! How can we be a family now? How can it be ok now?!"

She was crying uncontrollably now. Mr. Nader shuffled clumsily down the sofa and embraced her. At first she resisted but then fell into his arms, hugging him back as if it would somehow anchor her. The thoughts and emotions swirling around her head were overwhelming, she needed something to hold onto or shed get lost in them.

Mr Nader repeated, "I'm sorry, I'm sorry," over and over again like a mantra. Tears pricked his eyes but he quickly blinked them away.

Kaylin gradually felt the emotions lessening slightly, although she still felt raw. She became conscious of her breathing and began trying to regulate it.

In the dull haze, she somehow remembered reading about panic attacks in a doctor's waiting room a few months ago. It said that breathing in through the nose and out through the mouth, counting all the time, somehow helped. That's what she tried to focus on now, her breathing. Slow, deep breaths. In through the nose, out through the mouth. In through the nose, out through the mouth.

Her lungs trembled every so often as she inhaled, like a child trying to stop crying and be a brave little girl for mummy.

Or daddy.

After only a few minutes - but what felt like hours - she calmed enough to be able to focus her thoughts. She withdrew from the embrace and looked at Mr Nader, who was unable to hide the redness in his eyes or the tear that had streamed down one cheek.

She spoke in a pitiful whisper.

"When did it happen?"

"This morning."

"Oh."

She tried to feel some emotion but strangely found that she couldn't. It was as if the rush of emotions had somehow cauterised her to any more.

His answer to her question was utterly meaningless, devoid of anything. What difference did it make when her father had died?

She started to wonder why she'd even asked the question. The answer didn't make her feel better, or worse. What was the point in even asking it? She wasn't even affected enough to say she felt indifferent. The only things occupying the space where her emotions had been were emptiness and a cruel – but merciful? - numbness.

"I wanted to tell you I'd seen him Kaylin, I really did. I even followed you to school on a couple of occasions so that

I could tell you that he was around, but I just couldn't do it. And even if I could have found the words, I'm a doctor after all and he was my patient."

Was.

There's that word again.

Kaylin watched as her visitor swallowed hard, the veins in his neck straining with the effort of doing something so routine, yet now so strenuous.

"I even thought about telling you when you stayed over, but then you got so worried about your mother that I couldn't do it then either. How could I tell you that your father was dying Kaylin?"

She looked into his eyes and in that moment some emotion returned to Kaylin. She realised she felt extremely sorry for Mr. Nader. He was in pain too.

Then, *all* of her emotions came flooding back, as though arriving through the floodgates that she herself had opened by allowing herself to feel pity. She felt physically weak and her shoulders slumped under the weight of all that she'd felt.

She was more confused than she could ever remember being. A moment ago she'd felt grief, then nothing at all, and then - as she looked at the man sitting before her - she felt an overwhelming sadness and pity.

And now? Now she was experiencing a million other emotions that she wasn't yet old enough to describe.

"Why... Did he tell you why he was an alcoholic?"

Mr Nader paused again.

"He started drinking after he and your mother split up. He managed to stop drinking though Kaylin, for quite a lengthy duration. He was doing very well as a matter of fact, but then he got involved with illegal drugs. I'm not sure how or even why, Kaylin. To be honest with you, he probably didn't even know why himself. But I do know one thing Kaylin. He loved your mother until the very end. I don't think he ever got over what happened between them."

Kaylin's head swam with information, knowledge she didn't want but at the same time craved more than anything. She felt a vague sense of strength coming from somewhere.

Kaylin the Warrior was rising up from the depths, trying to take control. The next question Kaylin asked was so cold and clinical, and delivered with such a total lack of emotion, that Mr. Nader looked totally taken aback.

In truth, it shocked Kaylin too.

"So what exactly *did* happen between my mummy and daddy to ruin all our lives, Mr. Nader?"

It was the first time she'd called him by his name. The silence between them was magnified by his ever-growing pause, like an abyss yawning ever larger. He seemed to be trying desperately to understand how and why she would ask that question, and in such a way.

Kaylin was also trying to work out what had come over her, and just whose voice had come out of her mouth.

"I think... It's probably... I think its best you ask your mother about that, Kaylin. I'm sorry, I don't think that... well, it's not really my place to comment. All I can say is that he wanted to meet you one day and explain everything to you, and he wanted you to know that he wasn't a bad person, and that he loved your mother and wanted to have a family. He wanted you to have this too."

Mr. Nader reached into his blazer and pulled out a small envelope.

"It's sealed, I haven't touched it. He gave it to me yesterday and wanted me to give it to you if... if anything happened to him."

Kaylin took the envelope. It was crumpled and tatty, and she wondered just how many times he'd practised taking it out of his pocket to give to her in the past twenty-four hours.

A thought occurred to her.

"What was his name?"

The coldness in her voice had gone, replaced by an almost apologetic tone.

"Robert," Mr. Nader said solemnly. "Your father's name was Robert."

This time his answer did mean something to Kaylin. She sat whispering the name, eyes fixed on some point in the distance. Once again, she heard herself talking but as if from a distance. She kept changing what she was saying, but *Robert* was always in there somewhere.

She whispered so softly that she wasn't even sure she was saying anything aloud, and wondered whether it was just in her head.

"That's Robert's daughter... Robert's girl... That's Robert's little girl... Kimberley, Robert and Kaylin... Robert's little girl... This is my mum, Kimberley, and my dad, Robert... My daddy Robert... Robert's little girl..."

In an instant Kaylin felt herself snap back into the room, her features hard, her voice oddly clinical again. The words she spoke were hers, just like the words in her head were hers, but they were disconnected somehow. She was just the mouthpiece, with no idea where the words themselves were coming from.

"And how did this Robert character die exactly?"

Mr. Nader cleared his throat, and Kaylin saw tears well up in his eyes. He'd always been a stoic figure, not an emotional person. Kaylin felt physically sick at what she'd just said and the effect it'd had on him. There was a look in his eyes as if he wasn't recognising the girl in front of him. His daughter's best friend, no less. He'd probably be wondering how Annika would respond in the same situation, although Kaylin knew he would never allow the same set of circumstances to befall his daughter.

Kaylin twitched her head in an attempt to rid herself of *that* voice and *those* questions. As if they would be flung from her mind if only she jerked her head aggressively enough.

"He was admitted to hospital last night. He had chest pains and respiratory problems. He's been very ill for a long time Kaylin. I think his body just couldn't stand anymore, so..."

Kaylin's eyes fell to the letter in her hand.

Her thoughts seemed to blur and she couldn't quite grasp any of them – was she angry, or sad?

Emotions were lolling around her head, drunkenly staggering between her conscious and subconscious, not sure where they should be. Not sure whether they should be let out and displayed, or kept safely locked in. There was too much new information swirling around.

What exactly was all this supposed to *mean* for her? And her mum?

A lightning bolt struck as she remembered the one person in all of this that she'd forgotten about.

"Does my mum know?"

"No. I haven't told anyone but you so far. I spent quite some time speaking with your dad Kaylin, and his wishes were for me to first speak to you and give you that letter, and then speak to your mother afterwards. It's what he wanted."

They sat in silence for another eternity. Kaylin staring at the letter, Mr. Nader watching the young girl intently as if trying to read her body language and facial expressions.

Kaylin knew he would want to help her through this, and that he probably thought her mum wouldn't be much help when she found out. Everyone knew Kaylin's mum had her own problems with auditions and castings and all of that, and they also knew she wouldn't be the most attentive of mothers even at a time like this.

Kaylin turned to Mr. Nader.

"Would you do something for me please?"

"Of course Kaylin."

He reached over hesitantly, then gave her hand a reassuring squeeze.

"Would you open the letter and read it to me? I don't want the words to come from my head, if you know what I mean. They'll get confused with the other voic-... I'd just rather that you said them because I don't know what this is going to say. Could you? Please?"

Mr. Nader hesitated.

"Kaylin, as a psychiatrist, my advice would be for you to read the letter yourself in order to confront it on your own terms. In the long run, this would probably be better for you."

He wiped his brow again.

"However," he continued, "you're a young adult Kaylin, so I don't want to treat you like a child. If you need me to read this for you, then I will. Maybe just take a moment to consider it."

Kaylin nodded her head. She knew that she wanted someone else to read the letter, it couldn't come from her. She'd heard enough horrors come from her own mouth – and mind – she didn't think she could take much more. Even if psychiatrists would disagree with her conclusion, it was what she needed right now.

Sometimes the wrong thing to do is the only thing that should be done.

She looked at her best friend's father. He was the closest thing that she had to a father figure in her life, surely he'd know that and not let her down?

"I'd..." she began, "I'd really like you to read it to me please."

He paused, but only for a second.

"Of course I will Kaylin. I'll read it to you."

He smiled at her but she felt there wasn't much warmth behind it. It was as if he was scared again.

Maybe even he doesn't want to know what the letter might say. What wounds it might rip open.

What Kaylin didn't know was that Mr Nader was genuinely concerned about what she might do as a result of the letter. There was something slightly unstable about her demeanour now, as though she was trying to decide which impulse to obey. It was as if a third presence had joined them in the room.

He took the letter from Kaylin and opened it with trembling hands.

"Dear Kaylin," he began, "if you are reading this that means I am no longer on this earth. At the moment I'm dying and I know that I am and I only hope we got to meet at least once before it happened. If we didn't then I am sorry, because I've thought about you every day of your life. I'm not sure what your mother has told you about me, and I'm not going to disagree with her, I'm sure you love her as much as I do. What I will say is that I loved her more than I have ever loved anybody, although I know that I would have loved you even more."

Mr. Nader looked up. Tears were streaming down Kaylin's cheeks.

"Shall I continue?" he asked gently.

She inhaled deeply, trying and barely succeeding to control her breathing again. After a few moments she felt slightly more composed. She nodded.

"Erm... would have loved you even more... I loved your mother, she loved me, but she loved her career even more. Sometimes people do things they regret, but it can be too late because the damage is done and it can't be fixed. I hope you understand what I mean. Ask your mother, I'm sure she'll tell you what happened between us. It's funny because just before I started writing this I was thinking about my first date with your mother. Something on the television reminded me of it. There was an artist who was very famous at the time, his name was Andy Warhol and your mother was in love with him! She thought he was cool and trendy and all of those things. Truth be told, so did I Kaylin! This man was an artist and had a lot of odd ideas. He once that one day everybody in the world will be famous for fifteen minutes. That was your mother's favourite line. I hope it's true, because your mother needs that fame more than most. I hope she gets it, I honestly do. She needs it more than most for some reason, but I'm sure you know that."

(Fifteen minutes.)

Kaylin's fists clenched.

(Is that what all of this comes down to? Fifteen minutes so someone can feel good? Is that why my life is like this? So mummy can be famous for fifteen minutes while everybody else suffers and dies on their own?)

Magma was rising in Kaylin, pulsing and pushing its way to the surface. Ready to erupt.

Mr Nader continued reading, apparently unaware of the time-bomb in his midst.

"I am not sure what else to write. I suppose that there's nothing really left to say. Don't make the mistakes that I made Kaylin. I'm not a bad person but I have made bad decisions that have led me to great difficulties in my life. Look after yourself and don't chase wild dreams and fantasies. Follow your heart, but keep your head too. I'm sorry for the way things have turned out Kaylin, and I hope that somehow, somewhere I got the chance to tell you that face to face before you received this letter. Love always, your dad Robert."

Mr Nader looked up at Kaylin and opened in his mouth to speak, before closing it again.

Kaylin saw her own reflection in the television, and realised just what he was seeing.

Her eyes looked vacant but furious, lifeless yet seething with hate. The eyes of a person who had died in the midst of a murderous rage, seemingly frozen with an eternal, wrathful glare. The voice returned, and this time it didn't feel as though it was coming from anywhere but Kaylin.

(Fifteen minutes.)

(Is a life worth fifteen minutes? Is my *life worth fifteen minutes?)*

(Is that what this is all for, fifteen fucking minutes on a fucking television screen?!)

Kaylin began crying, but she was feeling far from weak. The rage was coming back stronger than ever now. Flooding her, overwhelming her completely this time. It overpowered any resistance she'd previously had.

Emotional blitzkrieg.

She'd felt something strange growing within her recently and that thing – whatever it was – had reached maturity. The gestation period was over.

The boiling ocean of rage and anger was being utilised and focused. She didn't want to kill or fight, but she did want something.

And, as Mr. Nader slowly folded up the letter and put it back in its envelope, she thought she'd figured out what it was.

Mr Nader told her that he'd sit with her until her mum came home, and would explain things to her directly.

Kaylin felt a jolt of adrenalin. She was looking forward to mummy getting home. She had a lot to answer for, it'd be nice for her to have to pay for her crimes in front of an audience.

Thirty One

David Haldane sat in his chocolate office.

It hadn't been a good day. The phone hadn't stopped ringing but it'd been nothing but crap. Nothing new on Andy the Artist, nor on any of the other stories he'd been chasing for that matter.

Nothing new on anything. It was becoming his trademark.

He'd woken up in the morning with an overpowering sense of frustration. The lead from the other day had got him nowhere fast – he hadn't learned anything that none of his competitors hadn't already known.

And as for other leads for other stories... They were as non-existent as his career was soon to be.

He began to wonder whether the naysayers were right, and that he was actually losing his touch. Maybe his detractors weren't being pessimistic or jealous, but were simply seeing things as they were. Maybe he was promoted too soon, like a boxer scheduled for fights he wasn't ready for. Or maybe the pressure had got to him along the way, and now he was folding. Crumbling like so many others he'd seen. Like so many others he'd ridiculed.

His wife had sensed his mood as he had dressed for work. He wasn't rushing as he usually did, and had dragged his feet at every turn. He'd even had breakfast before leaving home.

"What's wrong David?" she'd asked him. "Didn't you sleep?"

They'd both known it was a stupid question but they both went through the motions anyway. He never slept much, his mind not having an 'off' switch like other people seemed to have.

"I'm fine," he remembered telling her. "I've got a lot on, that's all. I'm fine."

He'd smiled what even he knew was an unconvincing grimace, and she had returned it with a gentle smile.

David knew she could tell that something was wrong, but he also knew they'd been married long enough for her to know when to give him time. He'd open up by himself when he was ready, she knew that. A good wife – and Gloria Haldane was indeed a good wife – would give him space, not nag him into submission.

David had always felt lucky to have her, often wondering – fearing – if that feeling was completely reciprocated. They'd been through a lot together. The fights, the redundancies, the attempts at having a child...

David's phone rang, bringing him back to his office with a start.

He looked at the phone, it was his private line. That meant it was important.

Good.

He couldn't be bothered for any more pseudo-important 'tips' about this bloody Artist case anymore, and he was fed up with having to field stupid questions from stupid people. Hopefully this call was something more useful than that tip from the other day, and from the day before, and the day before, and so on back into infinity.

He needed to get the exclusive on this Artist thing. His job, his way of life, depended on it. He had people all over the place hunting for snippets of information, hopefully his faith, and money, had been well invested.

He picked up the phone.

"David Haldane, can I help you?"

"Hello Mr. Haldane. I believe you're a fan of mine."

It was a woman's voice. Husky but not in a sexy way, there was definite harshness to it.

"Excuse me?"

"Tune into channel 84 on the UHF band, Frequency 910MHz, and you'll see what I mean."

"What are you talking about? How did you get this number?"

"Mr. Haldane, we don't have much time. As we both know the police are looking for me."

"Who are you?"

"Andy. Andy the Artist."

David Haldane brought a hand up and massaged his throbbing temples. He paused for a second, then something snapped in him and he gave full rein to his anger.

"You're the Artist, are you?" he spat into the phone. "Listen to me, don't waste my time you silly bitch! I've got more important things to do. Fuck off."

He slammed the phone down, shocked at his own lack of professionalism.

He closed his eyes and allowed his neck muscles to relax, leaning his head back. It was all getting to him, it really was. He had to be careful he didn't act like that in front of anyone important, or even among the lower levels in the newsroom. The knives were out for him, this is just what they'd be looking for to take to management and finish him.

He wondered what his next move should be. Shouting at strangers wasn't the answer though, he knew that much.

The phone started ringing again. He stayed in the same position with his eyes still closed, trying to block out the sound. The insistent ringing drilled deeper and deeper into his head with every ring.

Determined to be more professional, he took a deep breath and picked up the phone.

"Ok, I don't know who you are but please just listen-"

"No! You listen to me David Haldane. You've been trying to ally yourself with me and link us together in the public consciousness. Well, I'm helping you to do that. Don't make a rash decision you'll regret."

David shook his head, trying desperately to keep calm. When he spoke his voice was quiet and measured.

"You are not Andy."

It was the turn of the person on the other end of the phone to explode now.

"Andy the Artist, David! Not Andy. Andy the Artist, or The Artist, but never just Andy. Not to you or anyone."

"Ok, fine. In that case, you are not Andy the Artist."

"How do you know David? How can you be so sure?"

"Andy the Artist is a man. Do you not read the papers? Do you not watch television?"

The anger began rising in David again. He was determined to not start shouting and hang up again – if nothing else this was a test of how well he could keep calm under pressure. He needed to be more professional. He even wondered whether this was some kind of *actual* test by his bosses to see if he was starting to crack up or not.

A thought occurred to him - how did this crank manage to get his private number?

"I do both, David Haldane. I read the papers. I watch television. And I also frequent certain internet websites to find the stars of my next film. It's amazing what Jessica put on Twitter. And Susie told me everything I needed to know to find her too – even giving me her location at different times of the day. Have I got your interest now, Mr Haldane?"

David's interest was piqued. The names of the dead actresses had obviously been all over the place, so it was no surprise that this person knew them. But there was something about the tone of the woman's voice that began to cause the hairs on the back of his neck to stand up.

"I suppose you think my actual name is Andy? That I was christened Andy T Artist, by sheer coincidence? Think about it David, what do you *really* know about me?"

Silence hung between them. In his mind David ran through police reports and tips he'd heard. They all referred to the Artist being a man. But why? Based on what? Surely it was just an assumption. As a newsman, he should've known better.

On the other hand, what if this phone call was a hoax? What if one of the employees really did want to make him look bad? Wanted to sucker him into something ridiculous so that they would be able to take something to management and show them how badly he's losing it?

"This is too absurd I'm afraid young lady. I just... There's no proof that..."

"There is proof David. UHF band, channel 84, frequency 910MHz. Do it. Do it now and you'll know if it's true or not. Maybe I'm a fake, but there's only one way to find out. But hurry, David. Neither of us have much time."

"Look, I -"

The voice exploded again.

"David! Do it now! You want to be part of this don't you? Well this is it. Not going to miss your big break are you...? Spend so long looking for it only to miss it when it's right in your face? I've done my research on you too Mr David Haldane. You need me. That's why you've offered money out of your own pocket to find me. Well, I can save you that money if you just do what I say. You've got nothing to lose by switching to the channel, but you might have everything to lose if you don't. You've got 15 seconds to decide. Do I need to tell you to make it count...?"

David sat, stunned, for a few seconds.

She was right. What was there to lose? If it was hoax, he'd find out immediately by switching to the correct channel. And if it was real?

If it was real then Mr David Haldane was about to be very famous indeed.

He looked up at the huge plasma screens above the massive sofa as if seeing them for the first time, then suddenly began scrabbling around for the remote control. He knocked a few newspapers to the floor, but it didn't matter. His desk was normally immaculate, but because of everything that'd been happening – or *not* happening, to be more precise – he'd started using it as something of a dumping ground.

Finally retrieving the remote control, he started switching the screens back on with one hand, while picking up the second phone on his desk with the other.

"Maggie! UHF 84, 910MHz please.... No, 9-10, not 90... Yes.... I realise that, could you please just do it. Feed it to my office. Plasma 4. Thank you."

David slammed down the phone, pointed the remote at the bank of screens and hit the correct button for plasma screen four.

He watched the picture slowly appear on the screen, a vessel dragged up from the blackest depths of the sea. The picture changed from a dark black nothingness into something out of focus, then clear, then all too recognisable.

David's midsection tightened around his guts, painfully squeezing his stomach and organs like some invisible boa constrictor.

On the screen was the image that had been transmitted not only all over the United Kingdom but also all around the world. The media-dubbed 'Artists' Studio', a dirty cell with an even dirtier chair placed in the middle. The murder videos had been sent to the press and broadcast internationally – albeit with the murders themselves removed from the footage. Although David knew that some 'specialist' websites were allegedly showing the full tapes with the murders included.

David had pored over every frame of footage, even trying - and failing - to find the full versions on the internet. He had spent countless hours in this very office studying every detail, every sound, every mote of dust floating into frame.

There was no mistaking it, this was the cell.

"It can't be..."

"Oh it is, David. And don't bother calling the police, this won't take long. Start recording now."

"Recording? I can't... I need to go to a different room for that. In this office I can only-"

"Then you better hurry up David. Thirty seconds this time. Two times fifteen. Go now."

David transferred the call to be held in CR8 – or Crate as it was more commonly known in the office - the nearest control room to his office set up to both receive and record a live feed such as this.

He hung up the phone, and ran.

As he passed Maggie he barked at her to find the same frequency and channel and put it through to Crate.

Slightly taken aback, she asked him which screen he wanted to see the picture on. His answer was short, and to the point.

"All of them!"

He burst through the doors of the control room, just as the cell flashed onto every screen from left to right like an horrific Mexican wave.

He slammed himself down into the central chair and pressed the button to enable the speakerphone.

"Hello? Um... The Artist?"

The Artist's voice boomed out at him through the speakers in the small room.

"Very quick David, I'm impressed."

As the voice echoed around the room, David fumbled with the keys on the console, desperately trying to press 'Record' and trying less successfully to keep his excitement in check. This was it. This was the exclusive of the decade.

Maybe the century.

"Have you begun recording?"

"Yes, yes I have."

"Good. Would you like to see what I look like?"

David Haldane choked out the word, "Yes."

This was it.

"Sit down David, if you're not already. I'm going to tell you a story. And I'm going to make you very famous indeed."

David heard a strange rustling from the other end of the phone.

"Can you hear me, David? Is the sound coming through the channel?"

"Yes."

"Good. Then you can hang up the phone."

He disabled the phone and realised all of a sudden that he was leaning forward in his chair, literally on the edge of his seat. He imagined the audiences at home when he broke the story, straining forward in their own seats, watching David Haldane's world exclusive.

A shadow fell across the floor of the cell as the Artist walked into frame, holding an alarm clock in one hand and a gun in the other.

Thirty Two

David watches as The Artist places the clock and the gun on the floor, pausing to turn the dials on the timepiece.

He wonders whether an alarm is being set, and if so, who for?

The Artist finishes adjusting the clock, and stands bolt upright, staring directly into the camera. Nobody who had ever seen the murder films had known that when the person onscreen stared into the camera, they were actually staring into a mirror. David doesn't know that the Artist, just like all the victims, is staring at a reflection.

The Artist speaks.

"I have fifteen minutes. And don't worry, I'll make it count."

A slight smile creeps across the Artist's face.

"Ten years ago I was someone else. A lot can happen in ten years, in fact a lot can happen in ten minutes. But I suppose anybody watching this will already know that. Right now, here, today, I am an Artist. I am the Artist."

The Artist pauses and David stares at the figure on the screen. The small but muscular young woman, standing defiantly as though prepared for attack.

He can see she looks like a fighter, in the way she holds herself and the way her eyes burn through the camera.

She has the gait of a person supremely comfortable with violence, and well able to inflict it.

But does that mean she is a killer?

The killer?

The Artist continues.

"Ten years ago there were a number of murders in London. Actresses were getting killed after being invited to bogus auditions. The case was cruelly dubbed the 'Dying for fame' case, not only by the media, but also by the public. I remember watching the coverage on the news, hoping that my mum wouldn't be involved, hoping that she'd be spared. She wasn't."

"My mother's name was Kimberley Bellos. And mine was Kaylin."

The Artist's hands clench into fists at this point, the knuckles turning painfully white. The pain does not register on the face above.

"I'm sure you all remember the case, it was shocking enough to make the news headlines on a number of occasions. Shocking enough to be deemed newsworthy by the voyeuristic, bloodthirsty press. David, I'm looking at you..."

The Artist winks at the camera, managing to look both playful and menacing all at once. David shifts uneasily in his chair.

"In total eight actresses were killed, and guess who the last victim was? My mother. Just in case you've forgotten the details of the case, I'll remind you. The killer, a man named Joe Cameron, set up auditions with these young actresses, promising riches and fame and all the associated little toys we all think we want. Then he waited for them, struck them from behind, dragged them to a room without windows, degraded and violated them, then stabbed them to death."

The Artist spits the words out, venom dripping from every one. A cold grin forms on her face.

"And the press just loved it."

The Artists' eyes burn through the television and into David. A crowd has grown behind him, people walking past the control room and recognising the familiar looking cell on the bank of screens. Some have walked into the room out of curiosity, others have stayed outside - watching through the thick glass - as though afraid of what might happen if they enter. But they all freeze when they realise what – and who – they are watching.

The Artist's voice booms from the speakers. Even the phones seem to have stopped ringing.

"No doubt there will be comparisons between myself and that...*man* who killed my mother all those years ago. But those comparisons count for absolutely nothing. Where he butchered and murdered, I was humane. More than humane if truth be told, because I gave them exactly what they wanted. I've followed the coverage of myself. I have seen it on television, on the internet, I have heard it on the radio, even on the train while listening to commuters talking about it all. Everyone has been talking about them. In short, I have done for them what they always wanted. I've made them famous. I have taken three young actresses and given them what they craved. What they would, and I'm sure *did*, sell their muddy little souls for."

The Artist, truly her mother's daughter, pauses for dramatic effect.

"Fame."

The Artist practically vomits the word at the camera, as though desperate to be rid of it.

"Fifteen minutes of fame to be precise. Mr. Warhol's oft-quoted phrase had to come true for them sooner or later. Or else what would they have become? I know just what they would have become. Desperate, poor, they would have had to sell their bodies to buy food for their neglected, destined-to-forever-be-second-best children. They would hang on to each and every word spoken to them by somebody with a business card just in case this was the person who was finally, *finally*, going to give them that elusive yet irresistible little word. It's not a coincidence that it's a four letter word that begins with F..."

"They craved fame and probably thought it was owed to them, that they were destined for it. Well I gave it to them. And I wasn't barbaric. I told them how long they had to act out their little death scenes, cry some tears and make some noise. Then I ended their lives with a bullet. Quick and clean."

"Before you start judging me, remember my mother didn't have that luxury. After a life spent selling herself, body, soul, heart, everything, she was used one last time. Beaten and abused. Then dismissed. Casually discarded like chewing gum that lost its flavour."

The Artist seems to deflate slightly, as though the memories are having a physically weakening effect. The voice begins cracking, as though the pain of ten years is trying to break through mind and into body.

"My mum died on 21st December. So did my dad. And so did I. Kaylin Bellos died that day. Three lives and the promise of a life together as a family were taken. And why? So that one of those lives could have a chance at being famous."

The Artist looks down. For a moment David thinks he sees a tear fall from her eye, although it could easily be a trick of the light, or just his imagination. The control room, silent as a funeral parlour, watches. All eyes on the Artist.

Suddenly her head jerks up, as though a thought that could no longer be contained is forcing its way out.

"I had to identify my mum in the morgue. The *morgue*! It's not natural for a fourteen year old girl to have to do that. I had to look at her battered, bruised face and body. Is that fame? Is it? There was an audience wasn't there? We were all looking at *her* weren't we?"

The Artist is shouting now. The face turns red as the memories pulse through the body, vying to be released, seemingly forcing the capillaries to the surface of the skin. Thick veins bulge from the strong neck.

"And let me tell you something else about my mum. She honestly believed it would fucking happen. Just like all the others. She believed - truly fucking believed - that one day she'd do it. Nobody ever tells these people it's not going to happen. Nobody ever tells them they're wasting their lives.

She took me to the cinema once and spent the whole two hours watching the audience! Not the film, the fucking audience. Watching their reactions I bet, imagining that *she* was the one making them smile, making them cry, making them happy, making them sad. Well she was *my* mum. She should've been trying to make *me* happy! Trying *not* to make *me* sad!"

The Artist is twitching, nervous spasms travelling through the body, jerking limbs and shaking fingertips. This time tears really do start streaming. Tears which are angrily smeared away by shaking hands. A lifetime of anger being released.

"She used to tell me what it'd be like when she was famous. Delusions! All of it, delusions! Just another person scrambling to get rich and successful by pretending to be someone else – off screen as well as on. Well she got on TV. *And* in the papers. So she got what she wanted. Why shouldn't my own cast of performers have got what they wanted? And why shouldn't I have been the one to give it to them? I gave people fame. Don't you think that's what mummy dearest would've wanted?"

"And what did I get David? Any ideas? No?"

The word shot from her lips like a bullet.

"Grief. And do you know what grief is David? Grief is the fucking idiot that crashes the party just when you're having the most fun. Grief is a virus – festering and lying dormant, then breaking through and decimating you, destroying you from the inside. It's the bite of a black widow, you never see it coming, you never get a hold of it, and it always gets away. But the bite itself remains, stinging and poisoning and bringing you to the brink of death. It's always there David, and it'll never let you go."

The Artist pauses and for the first time David can see how this slight young woman could be a murderer. She is consumed, possessed.

She is The Artist.

"That's all I was left with David. A fucking wound that I managed to grow a scab over, which got ripped off over and over again, not only reopening the wound but shearing the skin around it. And it's even more painful each time because like a fool you allowed yourself to believe that it was healing. But it never heals David. You can't wait to be helped, you have to help yourself."

Kaylin breaks down. Her knees buckle and she crouches, crying tears for the lives ruined a decade ago, as well as the ones she'd taken. David stared with his mouth open.

She'd been consumed by rage for so long, what was left of her now?

Back in the control room one of the interns, a young boy named Nathan, rushes in to say the police have been called.

"What difference does it make?" David asks him bluntly. "They might trace the feed but how long do you think that'll take? She's got a *gun* Nathan, what do you think she'll do when the alarm goes off, wait for them to arrest her?"

Nobody's eyes dare move from the screen as the figure stands up and composes herself. She stands with her eyes closed, breathing deeply and slowly.

Once her breathing has regulated, Kaylin's eyes open and the Artist continues.

"So where does this leave us? Well, three lives for three lives, I think that's fair. Oh, and David, do you want to know what's hilarious? What's actually *funny*? Even though I used the same name – Joe Cameron – they still believed I was genuine. Ok, so they may have heard of Joseph Cameron from ten years ago, rather than Joanna Cameron from the here and now, but what difference does it make? All the *signs* were there. I used the same fucking name! It just shows they weren't paying attention to *reality*. Their minds were on their acceptance speeches and television appearances, not their lives. Their real, day to day, *lives*."

The Artist starts laughing through the tears.

"And do you know what else? They put up all their information on the internet! Names, dates, photos, where they went to school, what they know, what they can do, some of them even provided home addresses and telephone numbers! On the *internet*! They give hourly updates about where they are and what they're doing, they take photos and show what they're eating, who they're with! Don't tell me these people weren't asking to be found, asking to be made examples of. Were they really that innocent? If stupidity is a crime then I don't think so."

The Artist is pleased with this statement, finishing it off with a slight grin.

What none of her current audience know, is that somewhere deep inside, Kaylin feels repulsed, but it doesn't matter. She doesn't really exist anymore, her mental protestations slowly suffocating under the grief and the hurt and the pain. In truth, she hasn't really existed for a long time.

"Out of the three women I chose, only one of them stood me up, forcing me to find someone new. But that's still only one! And no doubt she'll now sell her story and get her fame out of me too. No matter. My mum got stood up much more than that, although that was probably because of the various bruises and cuts she kept getting from whoring herself out to strangers. Don't worry about that though, she was always getting hurt. We're resilient people us acting folk, don't worry, we'll be ok. Well, some of us will."

The Artist winks again.

David notices the figure on the screen fidgeting more and more. Her thought process seemingly becoming increasingly disturbed. Anger, then tears, then laughter, then more anger.

David feels restless too, his leg involuntarily shaking up and down. He knows what will happen once the alarm clock rings. So does everyone else in the room. The inevitably of the broadcast hangs in the air like a poisonous cloud, with nobody knowing how to stop it. Or even whether they should try.

"I know what you're thinking . *Is this the point where she kills herself? Is this where the villain of the piece escapes punishment?* Well I can assure you I've already been punished. The difference is that my punishment came *before* my crimes – if you really want to call them crimes. Because of my entire life and the way it's been up until this point, as far as I'm concerned I'm allowed to do *anything*. My punishment has happened already, don't doubt that for a second."

The Artist pauses, the years of strain showing on her face. The face of an eighty year old on the body of a twenty-four year old.

She sighs.

"And am I really guilty of anything that big? These women....I've done them a favour. Instead of living another miserable thirty years flirting with old men, not sleeping because they're worried about their career, doing terrible jobs with terrible pay, and so on and so fucking on. Instead of all that, instead of not being able to provide for their kids and eventually realising that the dream won't come true, instead of all that, I've made them famous. I've fulfilled their ambitions for them. I've made them something. They got their fame before they died, which is more than can be said for the millions of others who'll die disappointed, used up and empty. Just like mummy dearest."

The Artist's eyes glaze over at this point, as though haunted by a memory. The memory is quickly blinked away and the Artist continues.

"I want you to look at this and see the point I'm making. This isn't about killing people for fun. This is about justice. Justice for all the people whose lives end up broken and wasted, because the thing they've been looking for all their life doesn't exist. It doesn't exist! Even when they get it it's not real! Doesn't anyone see? Why else would rich and famous people commit suicide? After all, they've got everything haven't they? It's a lie! Show them this video David! Make them know it's a lie!"

The venom spewing from the Artist all of a sudden vanishes, replaced by an almost genial, friendly manner. Another dramatic mood swing. Truly her mother's daughter.

"And so ladies and gentlemen... You've been a great audience. I'm glad you've followed my work. No doubt a film will be made, portraying me as some kind of psycho. And I bet someone wins an award for playing me too, you know how audiences love the baddies!"

The Artist bends down and picks up the gun, as if anticipating the ringing of the alarm clock.

"It's nearly time. You know how this is going to end by now don't you? The alarm goes, then so does the villain of the piece."

The Artist stands up and releases the safety catch on the gun. The click is surprisingly loud, ricocheting around the barren walls of the cell. David wonders if this is the same gun that had killed all the others in this very place.

"Did I make it count, David? What do you think? Did I?"

To his, and everybody else's' surprise, David nods. He feels an overwhelming sadness for the figure he is watching on the screen. An empathy of sorts for this young woman whose crimes he had been so tirelessly following. This young woman, this wasted life.

But, at the same time, what had she done? She herself had taken lives, had destroyed families. And for what? What had she done it for?

As if reading his thoughts the Artist takes a step closer to the camera and speaks a single word.

"Justice."

Her voice echoes around the cell, echoes around the control room. And will soon echo around the world.

The alarm rings.

The Artist registers the noise with a tight smile.

The Artist.

Kaylin.

Daughter of Robert and Kimberley.

Best friend of Annika.

Serial killer.

She raises the gun and aims it at her head.

The alarm stops, the sound echoing away into nothingness.

Nobody in the control room dares to move. All eyes are on the screen.

The Artist slowly lowers the gun back down to her side, as if having second thoughts. Her eyes flick up to the camera, but they are unreadable.

Nobody in the control room dares to breath. David feels the sweat pricking at his brow and the back of his neck.

The figure on screen stares into the camera, her eyes focusing as if a decision has been made.

She brings the gun back up to her head and pulls the trigger.

Thirty Three

Chaos breaks out in the control room – phones are dialled, screams and shouts are heard - but only for a second. Just until it registers that there had been no gunshot, merely the click of an unloaded gun.

The figure onscreen is laughing now. She drops her hand back down to her side and ambles over to the chair in the centre of the cell. She sits down.

"Here's the thing. I did toy with the idea of loading the gun, but then I realised, the Artist is already dead. The Artist died the second I walked into this cell with a camera on me. I don't need bullets. How do you kill that which can only exist in anonymity? You destroy its cover. And how do you do that? What do you thrust upon it? David, you know the answer, you've been chasing it yourself recently. I'll give you a clue, it begins with F..."

In the control room all eyes turn to David, still sat in the centre chair, his forehead dripping with sweat and his heartbeat still painfully rapid. His eyes are on the screen, staring into the eyes of the figure inhabiting the cell, as he answers the question.

"Fame," he whispers, as the same word booms from the lips of the Artist, ricocheting around the control room.

"The Artist is dead, David. Three lives for three lives, and a load of collateral damage. Like my old friend Anni, or the life I could have had with my parents – ##both# of them – until it all got snatched away. The show's over, David."

She throws the gun on the floor of the cell.

"And as for me? I have ensured that the rest of my life will be as hidden as possible. I have ensured that if I ever seek fame I will suffer the consequences. I can now never fall into the trap my mother fell into. If I choose to have fame, anywhere in the world, I will be arrested. Kaylin is dead, the Artist is dead, and I'm what's left."

Her voice breaks as she says this, the message clear to all – there is nothing left. Her head is bowed and she wrings her hands, just as Annika's dad had done all those years ago. For a second the killer becomes the scared schoolgirl again.

She stands up and the chair pushes back slightly, the harsh scraping noise startling her and causing her to jump.

David can see that the figure onscreen is broken.

She looks back at the camera, her voice much lower now.

"Well, I hope you've enjoyed yourselves. The police should be arriving soon, although by the time they get to the correct location I'll be gone. You don't plan something for ten years then fall at the last hurdle by not investing in the right hardware. Rerouting a live feed is surprisingly easy once you work it out. Plus, when the police do eventually get here there'll be nothing left. Although that would be true even if I was still standing here, I suppose..."

She bends down and resets the alarm clock.

"Guess how many minutes until the device detonates?"

She smiles, and then laughs as she walks to the open door of the cell. She stands in the doorway and gives a friendly wave.

"Wish me luck!"

The cell door slams hard against its metal frame, the sound deafening in the control room. Three seconds later the screens are filled with white noise as the feed is cut. The transmission has ended.

The show is over.

Thirty Four

Kaylin was lying on her bed.

It had been a full day since she'd been told about her mum, and she was numb.

Kimberley had been missing for fifty agonizing hours before her body had been found.

Kaylin had been inconsolable when she'd been told, although she knew that she felt somehow angrier about the sad details of her father's life and death. He was more like her, an innocent victim. Whereas Kimberley - she'd almost brought this on herself.

I told her to be careful. I tried to warn her.

I should've been the one to finally put her out of her misery. On my terms.

I should've put her down.

The voice in Kaylin's head no longer felt alien to her. It was her new voice now. The other voice was rapidly dying, soon to be completely dead.

Just like her dad.

Just like her mum.

And, soon, just like Kaylin.

She'd been told the news by Mr. Nader. There was almost a morbid humour in the fact that he'd somehow been nominated to tell her about the death of both her parents.

Especially as he was a psychiatrist, because he'd know that she'd forever associate him with bad news. Which would mean forever associating Annika with bad news, so that every time Kaylin would look at her she would go back to *that* day. She would get *that* feeling.

Which would mean she'd have nobody left.

Mr. Nader sat in the other room.

Just in case the poor little orphan decides she can't take it anymore?

She'd had what would later be described as an 'episode' when she'd found out about her mum. She had ransacked the flat - emptying drawers, smashing her mum's perfumes, breaking the television. The rage took over and for the first time in her life Kaylin couldn't restrain it. And didn't feel like she particularly wanted to.

She didn't even know who she was anymore, but she knew she was different. And she knew that Kaylin was never coming back. Kaylin Bellos was as dead as her parents.

She'd completely decimated her mum's room, ripping up her clothes and emptying drawers all over the floor.

It was while she'd been doing this that she had stumbled across something in the bottom of the wardrobe. It was a Christmas gift from her mum, loving wrapped and hidden away, probably so as not to ruin the big surprise on Christmas Day.

She'd taken it and held it in her hands until now, where she rested it on her stomach as she lay on her bed. Her eyes were sore from crying, her face red and puffy. Her mind flashed back to her mum's bruised face before she died, then to the new cuts and bruises at the morgue. She didn't shake her head to get rid of the thoughts this time, that had stopped working twenty-four hours ago.

She read the card again.

"Dear Kaylin, love always, Mum."

The rage surged through her body, racing through her arms, forcing electrical impulses through her muscles.

Open this. Get it over with.

Now.

She clawed at the cheerful wrapping paper, tearing it to shreds in moments.

Underneath the paper was a plain white, soft-cardboard box. She ripped through the thin covering and looked at the gift inside.

It was an alarm clock.

A yellow egg-shaped thing with a purple face. On top was what looked like a miniature fried egg.

There was a small card inside. The writing was her mum's – 'Happy Christmas Kay! Now you've got no excuse to not be on time!'

Time...

Kaylin began to weep, then cry, then wail. Her eyes closed and she saw images from her old life, images of her mum, of what could have been. As the images fell into her mind, the tears fell from her eyes.

I'll make it count, mum.

I know what I want now.

Justice.

She opened her eyes. They were dead now, and her face was a mask.

Hatred. Rage.

She stared, not into the distance this time, but into the future.

Looking, scouring, hunting.

I'll put them down.

I'll put them all down.

A smile creeps onto the Artist's face.

I'll make you famous...

Dear Reader,

Thank you for reading my debut novel ***The Artist****. I hope you enjoyed it, and I sincerely hope you didn't guess the twist at the end...*

I wrote this book after realising how much information I was putting online as an actor and comedian, and subsequently how easy it would be for somebody to track me.

I was also becoming jaded with the whole process of getting gigs and going to auditions, so I put these elements together - with a bit of murder thrown in, of course - and The Artist was born.

I would love to hear any feedback you might have, so please do get in touch either through my website at ***www.angelomarcos.com****, or via email at* ***info@angelomarcos.com****.*

(Yes, there I go telling people how to find me again...)

As an independent author I also genuinely value – and always need! – reviews, so if you have a couple of minutes I'd really appreciate you putting a review up online.

Lastly, if you've enjoyed this book then you might also like my psychological thrillers ***Victim Mentality*** *and* ***Sleep No More****. Please see the next page for more information.*

Thanks again for reading!

Angelo

Victim Mentality by Angelo Marcos

Sleep No More by Angelo Marcos

They started as nightmares, vivid terrors striking in the darkest recesses of the night.

The faceless shadow form, chasing Ariadne Perasmenos through her dreams.

Finding her, subduing her. Slaughtering her.

But now things have changed.

The nightmares have started to leach into reality, their grip extending way beyond the subconscious realm.

The line between what is real and what is not becomes increasingly blurred as Ariadne finds herself waking up bruised and bloodied.

But is the 'Shadow Man' real, or a figment of her imagination? Is she being hunted by some demonic creature, or suffering from some psychological disorder?

Seeking the truth, and unable to trust herself , Ariadne is in a deadly race against time.

Because the next time she falls asleep, she might not wake up again...

Sleep No More is available in both ebook and paperback formats

Copyright information

THE ARTIST
ISBN-13: 978-1479319275
ISBN-10: 1479319279